ABRIELLE

JACK BERNARD RHODES

Copyright © 2024 Jack Bernard Rhodes.

All rights reserved. No part of this book may be reproduced, stored, or transmitted by any means—whether auditory, graphic, mechanical, or electronic—without written permission of both publisher and author, except in the case of brief excerpts used in critical articles and reviews. Unauthorized reproduction of any part of this work is illegal and is punishable by law.

ISBN: 979-8-89419-545-2 (sc)
ISBN: 979-8-89419-546-9 (hc)
ISBN: 979-8-89419-547-6 (e)

Because of the dynamic nature of the Internet, any web addresses or links contained in this book may have changed since publication and may no longer be valid. The views expressed in this work are solely those of the author and do not necessarily reflect the views of the publisher, and the publisher hereby disclaims any responsibility for them.

One Galleria Blvd., Suite 1900, Metairie, LA 70001
(504) 702-6708

CONTENTS

Chapter One 1
Chapter Two 6
Chapter Three.. 11
Chapter Four.. 14
Chapter Five..24
Chapter Six 28
Chapter Seven 33
Chapter Eight..39
Chapter Nine 43
Chapter Ten 48
Chapter Eleven..53
Chapter Twelve 58
Chapter Thirteen 69
Chapter Fourteen 79
Chapter Fifteen 84
Chapter Sixteen...88
Chapter Seventeen...91

Chapter Eighteen 95
Chapter Nineteen 98
Chapter Twenty 101
Chapter Twenty-One 107
Chapter Twenty-Two 112
Chapter Twenty-Three 123

CHAPTER ONE

Wilder Kanazawa nervously opened the door to the maternity ward. He walked slowly to where his wife, Bethany lay, holding their newborn. He leaned over to touch her tiny fingers. They were overjoyed to finally receive the blessing of a beautiful baby girl after trying for so long. They were excited about the much needed change in their lives. Abrielle's parents had cherished her above all things, and she could always rely on their undivided attention.

Four years later, Claudia was born, which changed Abrielle's world. She felt her new sister had taken the shine away from her. She no longer had the sole care of her parents. She could no longer do the things she had always taken for granted, anytime she pleased. She couldn't sleep with her mother whenever her father was out of town on business like she used to. She had to take turns with Claudia. She could no longer sit on the couch between her parents at night fot it was just the three of them. Claudia was always there too and stealing affection away from her. Abrielle raged with jealousy when Claudia breastfed. She felt neglected whenever her sister was coddled by their parents or anyone else. Abrielle was losing her parents to Claudia, or at least, that's what she had convinced herself. To punish her parents, she would often withdraw from them for spending time with Claudia. Abrielle hated her and wished she was never born.

The stench of diaper changing and the sight of the fecal matter disgusted Abrielle. She had to share her bedroom with Claudia, and It wasn't enough that she had to tolerate her little sister's crying spells during the night. When their mother came into the bedroom to check on Claudia, she would ignore Abrielle. Because of Claudia, Abrielle felt she was not only less loved; she was becoming invisible. So, she created a fake illness almost daily to drag her mother's attention away from Claudia.

Abrielle was bent on revenge and looked for ways to get it. She taunted Claudia when alone with her. Whenever their mother put her in the playpen and left the room, Abrielle would slap her leg, poke her arm and squeeze her hand until she cried. She would always pretend to comfort Claudia when their mother rushed back into the room.

Time passed, and when Claudia was four years old, she picked up one of Abrielle's dolls, who forbade her from touching. She dropped the doll when she heard

Abrielle shout and ran inside the bedroom closet. Standing at the entrance where her younger sister was hiding in terror gave eight-year-old Abrielle a sense of dominance. Her jealousy raged as she leaned forward. With a kitchen fork, she jabbed her sister's knee, leaving four bloody prick marks. Abrielle was frozen with shock at Claudia's screams of pain and realized that she had gone too far in tormenting her sister.

"What have you done?" Bethany shouted at Abrielle as she picked up Claudia. "Look at this! Your sister's knee is bleeding! What has gotten into you?"

"I'm sorry!" Abrielle, who was then crying, pleads with her mother.

Bethany sat Claudia on the bed, grabbed Abrielle's arm, and led her out of the room. She whacked her daughter's rear several times in the hall with her open hand. "Don't you ever hurt your sister again! Do you understand?" Abrielle could only nod as she let out a loud, harsh cry.

Abrielle stewed as she watched her mother rush back to pick up Claudia and comfort her. Bethany carried her youngest daughter to the bathroom to treat her wound with a first aid antiseptic as Abrielle followed.

"Go back to your room and stay there! I'll deal with you later!" Abrielle's mother said to her sternly. She scampered back to her room, but she could still hear her mother comfort Claudia in baby talk, and this inwardly enraged her.

At supper time, Abrielle watched her sister as she sat on her booster seat. To Abrielle, Claudia seem to be getting all the attention from their parents that should be rightfully hers. She panicked when her father examined Claudia's knee. She was hoping the fork incident would be forgotten by the time he had got home from work. He gave Abrielle a cross expression as he sat to eat but said nothing about it. She had relaxed through the meal, thinking the coast was clear. She asked to be excused, but her father told her to stay seated. He calmly asked her why she jabbed her sister with a fork, although he and Bethany were aware of Abrielle's jealousy of Claudia. After no answer, he asked if she was having problems at school. She shook her head as she looked down at her plate. He wondered if anything was bothering her that she wanted to discuss. She said there wasn't, but she gave an anguished expression as she looked over at her sister.

"Abrielle, your sister is only four years old. There is no reason for you to resent her. We love both of you equally," explained her father.

"You're both very precious to us," her mother added.

"Don't ever hurt Claudia, again. Have I made myself clear?" Her dad waited for a response. "Abrielle, answer me. Do you understand?"

Abrielle finally looked up at her father and glared at him. It was more than a look of defiance. It was *perverse.* "Yes, sir," she said, but her tone gave her mother a chill and outraged her father. He got up from the dining chair as if to grab Abrielle.

"No, Wilder!" Bethany shouted for him to stop.

"Go to your room, Abrielle!" Wilder restrained himself and took a deep breath.

CHAPTER TWO

"Stay out of my room while I'm gone, you little twerp!" Demanded Abrielle as she prepared for her date.

"Oh sis, I don't care about anything in your room. Relax," replied Claudia. "I'm leaving too. I have youth choir practice tonight.

"Don't call me *sis!* You know I hate that!"

"I'm teasing you, Abrielle. I'm sorry. I know you don't like that name but would you please not call me a twerp?"

"Well, if the shoe fits." Abrielle sneered.

"It's raining, Claudia," Bethany announced. "I'll drive you to choir practice."

"That's ok, mom. I'll use an umbrella. I can still walk. Unless you and Sabastian would drop me off, Abrielle?" Asked Claudia.

"No way! There's no time. He'll be here any minute. We want to get a good seat before the movie starts," Abrielle responded angrily.

"The church is on the way to the movie. Dropping your sister off is not going to cause a delay," Their mother snapped back.

"Your sister this and your sister that! Sister, sister, sister! Everything centers around my little sister!" Ranted, Abrielle.

"All right, young lady!" Said Bethany. "You'll not go anywhere with that attitude!"

"Look! It's not raining all that hard. I'll just walk." Claudia offered in an attempt to keep the peace.

"We'll drive you there, Miss goodie-two-shoes," Abrielle quipped. "I wouldn't want you to get wet."

Hearing the phone ring, Abrielle answered it, suspecting Sabastian calling. "Sabastian Cassworth, where are you?"

"I'm leaving now. I'll be there as soon as I can." He responded.

"Well, if you're going to be late, don't bother coming!" She slammed the receiver down and cutting off the line. Ten minutes later, Sabastian was knocking on the front door.

Abrielle opened the door with a scowl. "We don't have much time! We need to take my sister with us and drop her off on the way. Hurry up, Claudia!"

"Thank you, Sabastian," Bethany said as she greeted him.

"No problem, Mrs. Kanazawa."

"Why don't you guys skip the movie and sit in on our choir practice instead? It'll be more entertaining than your movie," offered Claudia. There will be finger food there. You both are welcome to come."

"That's not happening. This is the last day to see *Pulp Fiction*. I'm not missing it!" Abrielle responded.

"Isn't that R-rated?" Bethany asked?

"Mom, I'm eighteen! Give me a break."

Sabastian was getting uncomfortable with the exchange. "Shouldn't we be leaving?"

"Oh, my god, it's a quarter after. The flick starts in fifteen minutes," Abrielle warned.

"Let's go. I'm ready," added Claudia.

As the three walked to Sabastian's car, he asked Claudia about her choir practice. The two talked all the way to the church.

"I notice how you keep looking at my sister in the rearview mirror," Abrielle said to Sabastian, confrontationally, after dropping off Claudia.

"Don't be silly! We were just having a discussion," Sabastian reasoned.

"Well, you conveniently left me out of your little discussion."

"We weren't stopping you from talking, Abrielle," laughed Sabastian.

"Just don't get frisky with me, in the movie, Mr. Laughing man!"

"Take it easy, beautiful. I don't care anything about your little sister. She's just a kid.

Abrielle loved it when Sabastian called her *beautiful,* and it lightened her mood, but she wasn't budging an inch. The first time they met, she detected his insecurities and knew he could easily be manipulated. She purposely would not clarify if she wanted to bewith him. She would blame everything on Sabastian and insinuate that their relationship cannot work with someone like him. She would demand that he do simple things that she could easily do herself. She would often make him aware of any of his traits that h was sensitive about. She would be loud and insulting with the purpose of having dominance over him. She would pretend to cry to make him feel uncomfortable. He would do everything he could do to make her stop crying. She would make him jealous byreminding him that he's not the only man around. She would use sex to control him. She planned to keep him on a string until she was done with him like she had treated all the others before him.

After their first date, when Sabastian met Abrielle, he was on cloud nine. He felt he was the luckiest guy in Detroit to find a girl as beautiful as her. He couldn't imagine life without her, and the thought of losing her was unbearable. He wanted to be seen with her and show her off to his friends. He even invited her to have dinner with his parents. This was something that he had never done before. She was very charming to everyone, and life, for him, was perfect, at first. Then she became increasingly moody, and it was making him uneasy. She was belittling him in front of others. She started putting down his friends and even his parents. Nonetheless, she had a hold on him. He talked to some very nice girls who showed an interest in him, but they couldn't do for him what Abrielle did. He was addicted to her sexually, but it was more than that. She was erotic beyond meaning. He was utterly and hopelessly under her spell. Lately, he fantasized about breaking things off with her. He wanted to resist her and berate her in front of others as she did him. He wished he could find the courage.

CHAPTER THREE

Claudia had a strong interest in her faith from an early age and prayed for her older sister, daily. Their parents tried, in vain, to shelter Claudia from the problems that had plagued Abrielle throughout her teen years. Claudia was aware of their father's trip to thepolice station where her sister was held when she was only fourteen. Abrielle was in a car with a boyfriend who was arrested for drunk driving. Claudia had endured her sister's angry emotions, including verbal and physical abuse. Claudia worried about Abrielle's rebellious behavior that included drug use. Claudia would pray for Abrielle's progress during every court-ordered trip to the therapist. Claudia loved her sister dearly. She had faith that Abrielle would change one day.

Claudia enjoyed school and excelled in academics. She moved ahead in her classes, which allowed her to graduate two years early and advance to college to study law. Due to accelerating in her high school grades, she was only one year behind Abrielle in school.

Abrielle's classmates and even the teachers raved about Claudia's academic performance. At home, their parent's attention was so totally focused on Claudia that it made Abrielle fiercely jealous, and she felt under constant pressure. She never had the aptitude to breeze through her classes effortlessly, like her younger sister. She studied diligently for her exams and made good grades but couldn't compete with Claudia's academic superiority. She felt invisible at home, inferior at school, and she blamed it all on Claudia. She felt there was little she could do to deal with it, so she looked elsewhere to vent her frustrations and find dominance. Then, she meets Sabastian. He was easy to control and intimidate. She had power over him.

After Abrielle graduated from high school, she didn't want to continue living with her parents, even just through the summer before leaving for college. She felt she couldn't tolerate their rules and constant adulation for Claudia. Likewise, pursuing a summer job didn't appeal to her. The thought of it irked her. She was confident in herself to get money without working for it. Sabastian was already out of college, had a great paying job, and lived in a lovely apartment. So, Abrielle decided to stay at his place as much as possible. She could easily manipulate him to suit her own needs. She spent his money and used his new red *Mustang* since her old *Ford Focus* was barely drivable. In the beginning, she used his car only on weekends, then pressed him to allow her to borrow it while he drove hers to work. He was afraid he would lose her if he said no. She had reminded him again that other guys would love to have her.

CHAPTER FOUR

Nicholas Xanders was irresistible to every woman he pursued. He first encountered Abrielle on a shopping trip at a mall while Sabastian was working. *That girl looks nice,* Nicholas thought to himself. As each was walking toward each other, she noticed, by his physique, that Nicholas took care of himself, and he was impeccably stylish in his wardrobe, too. They made eye contact, and he winked. It was an indescribably suave and smoky wink that was pure sexy. He also had a natural, masculine scent that drove Abrielle wild.

Later that day, Abrielle didn't return Sabastian's car after he arrived home from work. She finally returned it at midnight and claimed she was with her girlfriend, who she hadn't seen in ages. "We were having a talkfest and forgot about the time," she lied. After that, her not returning his car until late was a regular occurrence. She didn't want a classy guy like Nicholas to know she drove an old and inexpensive vehicle. Sabastian demanded she stop such behavior that always turned into an argument that rarely ended well. He was tempted to take his car keys away but feared her wrath. Ending their relationship was out of the question, for he loved her and couldn't bare the thought of her leaving for good. He was powerless against Abrielle.

She loved the security and dependability that Sabastian provided. These were needs Abrielle didn't think she would ever have with Nicholas, whose secretive behavior made her leery of him. He received multiple phone calls from acquaintances whenever she was with Nicholas, who he wouldn't reveal to her. He shared little about his personal and business affairs. She suspected that she wasn't the only one he saw, but she was drawn to him. He had a mysterious way that was hard to explain. He was gaining more control over Abrielle as the weeks passed. He was highly self-absorbed that she misinterpreted as arrogance but later discovered he was genuinely superior over other men.

He was apparently wealthy, for he lived in a spacious and lavish apartment in a ritzy area. Nicholas drove a new Bentley Continental GT, and she knew it was a more expensive car. She was shocked to discover its worth was over $200,000 when she researched the car's make and model. He had a quintessential air of self-confidence, and he was the most intelligent man she had ever met. Sabastian continued to have tolerance as they saw each other less and less. She would create the deception that she was out with girlfriends or family.

Nicholas took Abrielle to new places such as concerts, art studios, museums, and extravagant restaurants. Several times, she had the feeling, which she couldn't explain, that strangers knew Nicholas but would never actually speak to him. It puzzled her, at first, that he only made himself available to her once or twice each week. Often, he was away traveling on business for days. He would say nothing, to Abrielle, about his livelihood, but one evening, when she pressed him on it, he invited her to a meeting. He promised the assembly would answer some of her curiosities, but he shared nothing else.

When Nicholas stopped in front of a large building several stories high, a well-dressed man helped Abrielle out of the car. "Show Abrielle to the guest section, Lawrence," Nicholas instructed.

"Yes, sir, Mr. Xanders."

"Aren't you coming, Nicholas?" Abrielle asked.

"Relax, Abrielle. I'll be there. Please, go with Lawrence, and he'll take care of you."

She entered a large auditorium and was in awe at the exotic potted plants, flowers, and even small trees that filled the stage and lined the walls. She was led to a box seat, where she sat alone. Below, over a thousand people sat quietly as soft music from a sound system played. The theater drapes opened to reveal Nicholas in center stage as he stood behind an acrylic and wood lectern. The audience stood to cheer and applaud. When he began to speak, they sat quietly and were practically motionless.

Nicholas spoke of love for each other and how it's the only law that each member of The Order of Xander's Disciples must be followed in attendance. This included all its members across the nation. He claimed that each "disciple" was excluded from all man's religious laws. They were required to love each other as his disciples and follow his direction through his contact with God. He told a story, as he had shared many times, how an unknown force mysteriously led him to travel to a remote desert region of Nevada. He drove through a scarcely trafficked backroad and stopped his car. He started walking and was suddenly possessed by a paranormal experience of soaring farther into the desert until he reached a plateau. It was there; he heard a thundering voice from the heavens, who could only be the God of all creation. The voice declared Nicholas as his messenger and messiah.

Nicholas continued describing the wonders of Xander's Disciples as the only true faith, while Abrielle began to experience a feeling of awakening. Her very existence was making sense for the first time. She was positive that everything throughout her life led her to this same night and in this auditorium.

* * * * * * * * * * * *

Abrielle's first college semester began soon, and her parents discovered she'd not yet registered. She had frequently been away from home all summer and was strangely distant whenever she was home. Her parents were justifiably concerned.

"What do you mean, you're not going to college?" Wilder asked his daughter, when she got home, late one evening. "We've been preparing your college career for years. Don't blow your chance!"

"Well, I have other plans," Abrielle replied tersely.

"You are making a mistake, honey," Bethany added. She reached over to hug Abrielle, but she pulled away and got up from her chair to leave.

"Don't throw your life away, Abrielle." Her dad shouted as she walked away.

"Please, don't walk away, honey," Bethany pleaded. "Go to college, sweetie. Claudia will be attending the same university next year, and you and she will be there together."

"Oh, here we go with Claudia, again!" Abrielle complained.

"What are your plans? Marriage? Are you and Sabastian planning to get married?"

"Sabastian? Ha! What a joke! I have better plans for my life." The following day, Abrielle packed her clothes and all of her belongings. She left home before her parents awakened and never returned.

* * * * * * * * * * * *

"She's not here. I haven't seen her in three days, and I don't know where she is," Sabastian told Bethany when she called.

"She packed her things and left four days ago," said Bethany." She didn't even say goodbye. We're worried to death. We don't know where to turn. Surely, she said something to you, Sabastian."

"Like I told you, Mrs. Kanazawa. She's not here, and I haven't heard from her! Everything was ok the last time I saw her. Something must have happened."

"Please, Sabastian. Call us as soon as you hear from her," pleaded Bethany.

Sabastian hung up the receiver and reflected on his maddening ordeals with Abrielle. He painfully recollected how she berated him, drained his bank account of thousands of dollars, took over his car, and controlled him. He still missed her and wanted her back. His heartbreak lasted for months. His depression led to years of therapy that ultimately helped him emerge from his denial and accept his reality.

* * * * * * * * * * *

Nicholas assured Abrielle that she was destined to prominence in the hierarchy of the divine order within Xander's Disciples. Through dedication and diligence, she would ultimately bask in the order's pleasures up to its inundated capacity. Nicholas explained that eventually, she could have authority over many within the order. What was even more alluring was that she could gain the ability to actually manifest misfortunes against anyone she chose. For her, it meant more power than she ever dreamed possible. It meant control over everyone who cheated her out of her happiness. It even meant control over her sister. She was determined to commit herself totally to the order and not allow anything or anyone to stop her. However, she must start at the bottom of the class structure. She must first experience a *rebirth.*

After dark, she was picked up to be driven to an undisclosed location by Lawrence, the same man who walked her to her seat during the first meeting. Once inside, a woman, with a pleasant manner, led her to a room with no windows but was tastefully decorated. She introduced herself as *Candace,* and showed Abrielle to a couch to relax, and then left the room. She was alone and tried to visualize ahead since nothing was revealed about day-to-day life that would follow.

Candace returned and handed Abrielle a dress that reminded her of pioneer colonial garb. "Take everything off, including your bra and panties. Change into this, sweetie," Candace instructed.

"You expect me to wear that ugly thing?" Abrielle said in protest.

Candace's mood abruptly changed. Her sweet-natured demeanor turned cold made Abrielle tremble. "Let's get one thing clear," warned Candace. "From this moment going forward, you will obey without question." She laid the dress over the couch and left the room once more. Ten minutes later, when she returned, Abrielle wore the pioneer colonial style dress. She folded her Gloria Vanderbilt jeans, V-neck pleated top, and underclothing. She placed them on the arm of the couch and nervously waited. Candace picked up the items, including Abrielle's purse. "Your items will be safely stowed. You will stay in this room until you receive further instructions."

"When will I get my clothes back?" Abrielle asserted.

"As I said, your items will be safe." Candace's cordiality was completely gone.

She sat in the room and was alone with her thoughts for what seemed to be an eternity. She felt vulnerable in the old fashion dress with nothing underneath. The change in Candace's mood had unnerved her, too. However, she thought it was too late to change her plans and go home to her parents. Candace had intimidated her enough, and Abrielle didn't want to antagonize her anymore by resisting. She felt shame, for she had never allowed anyone to cause her to experience such fear. She closed her eyes and thought about what Nickolas had said about the splendor of the Xander society. The thought helped her relax and renew her confidence.

Candace was fully dedicated to the order for the past twenty years. She had been through the same mental conditioning or rebirth as Abrielle was about to digest. Candace robotically served at the compound seven days a week, all those years, with no social or family life. She would think about the grandeur she was promised initially, but it would never be. She still considered it an honor to be part of the order in any fashion. It was the only life she knew. She was painfully aware that nothing on the outside was waiting for her.

Private Detective Hunter of Target Investigative Agency, was befuddled as he depleted the last of a long list of leads in the search for Abrielle Kanazawa. It was a marathon investigation in comparison to the more common cases of child custody cases, serving papers, surveillance and tailing targets. When her family hired him over a year ago, he assured them speedy results, but it was as if she vanished into thin air. He had interviewed all the people she last contacted. He worked closely with the police on their missing person investigation. Neither the cops nor Hunter's agency could find a trace of her whereabouts.

Claudia sat in her college dorm room, pondering the whereabouts of her missing sister and how it was tearing the family apart. She should be enjoying the best years of her life while attending the university. However, with Abrielle missing for almost two years, Claudia feared the worst. As she had been doing every night, she bowed her head and prayed for Abrielle's safe return.

Abrielle was allowed to stand outside the compound for the first time in what must have been many months. For exactly how long, she didn't know. There were no windows to savor daylight and no clocks either. She was told when to eat, sleep, and even use the bathroom. She was deprived of sufficient food and sleep if she dared question anything. She lived by the daily rules of the order and the immensity of its superiority above all else.

CHAPTER FIVE

Wilder and Bethany sat across the desk of Police Detective Gilbert Westbrook. He reminded them that it had been seven years since their daughter had been missing. All the leads had been exhausted, and he warned there was no reasonable hope that new information would come to light.

"There is no evidence that your daughter is still alive, but there is no evidence to support she is dead either," expressed the detective. "I can keep the file open unless you have considered declaring your daughter dead in absentia?"

"Dear God, no!" Shouted Bethany.

"We will never do that," added Wilder. "It's out of the question. Please, continue the search. We know she's out there."

She reflected back to the night, long ago, during the first assembly she attended. Until that night, Abrielle was unaware that she was in an intimate relationship with the one and only true messiah, Nicholas. Thanks to his ultimate wisdom, she was put through an elevated rebirth reserved for a select few. It far exceeded the usual exaltation of the overwhelming majority of the disciples in the order. She was indoctrinated with the belief that she had superhuman abilities. She was to love all of the disciples within the order and never use her powers against them under any circumstances. However, the great masses outside the order referred to as the "damned" would be subjected to her will.

* * * * * * * * * * * *

Claudia was having classic symptoms of pregnancy. Her breast was sore, she was tired all the time, and she had missed her period. She was almost sure of the results but waited until after her pregnancy test before telling her husband, Brent. They had been married for three years.

When her doctor informed her that the pregnancy test was positive, she wanted to shout to the world that she was having a baby. She still had a long day ahead, in meeting clients and preparing court cases at her private law practice. Later, she would tell Brent, the news, when she got home and call her parents that night.

She finally got through the day and picked up some special groceries for dinner that evening to celebrate her pregnancy. Brent hadn't yet arrived when she got home, so she called her mother. She was excited and couldn't wait to talk to her.

When Bethany answered her phone and heard Claudia's voice, she immediately started crying.

"Mother! What's wrong?" Claudia asked in dismay.

"Your dad and I are just upset about our talk with Detective Westbrook earlier today. All the leads to finding your sister have been exhausted. It's hard to believe that we reported her missing seven years ago on this very day.

"I know, Mother. Please, don't give up hope," consoled Claudia. Given the length of time, there wasn't much more she could say. She still prayed for Abrielle every day. "I have some good news."

"What dear," her mother asked.

"I had a pregnancy test today. You're going to be a grandmother!"

"Oh, my God! Really, Claudia? Are you sure?"

"Absolutely, and it's a girl!"

I got to tell Wilder! Hold on! Wilder, we're going to be grandparents!" Bethany shouted.

"Well, hallelujah! It's about time!" Wilder shouts back jubilantly. He raced out of the den, and Bethany handed him the receiver. "We'll all go celebrate tonight!"

"Not tonight, Daddy. I haven't even told Brent yet. I'm waiting for him to get home. I'm making a special dinner for just the two of us. Well, three of us, actually," she laughed. I'm going to tell him over supper. We've been so anxious to have a baby."

"We have to! We'll all have to do something special this weekend."

"It's a deal, Daddy!"

* * * * * * * * * * * *

After seven years, Abrielle was on the brink of completing her duties in the compound. The exclusive conditioning of the newest disciples that she assisted demanded constant discipline. Each day of her service in the order gave her an increased, false sense of empowerment. She was delusively taught to believe, through her sheer will, that she would have the abilities to control the course of anyone's life outside the walls of the compound. She would soon be leaving.

CHAPTER SIX

Nicholas instructed the compound to exclusively submit month-by-month updates on Abrielle's progress. He demanded her weaknesses to be turned into strengths. She was driven to her absolute limits.

Abrielle had achieved the top-echelon of rebirth within the order. Nichola's supreme plan would soon be a reality. He would introduce Abrielle as his new queen of Xander's Disciples. It was only a formality to portray a sense of family authenticity within the order. Nicholas conceived that a queen would multiply the membership across the globe.

She was picked up at the compound by a chauffeur in a *Century-Royal*, a limousine befitting her new status. She was driven for hours to her destination. The driver parked in front of a 10,000 square foot, *Greek Revival-style*home. It had been converted into the official Xander's Disciple's headquarters, where daily tasks were implemented within the order. Nicholas and his staff walked out to greet Abrielle.

Little time was wasted. Abrielle spent all of the following day in photo sessions to be viewed by the followers. Nicholas introduced Abrielle, Queen of the Order of Xander's Disciples, in a recording. The recording was sent to all of the hundred thousand disciples, and Abrielle was a sensation. Each member was sworn to secrecy and did not reveal anything about the order to the masses or the *damned* as they were referred to.

Nicholas and Abrielle were doing tours of all the cities where the order had the most significant following. They both made eloquent speeches about the greatness of the order. They expressed how each disciple was part of their messiah's unique people, and they were to love one another. They spoke of how the damned were perverted multitudes and mere, lower-class beings.

After her first round of tours, Abrielle was confined to the disciple's headquarters and not permitted to leave. The household staff cared for all of her needs and typically there was little for her to do. This left plenty of time to think about her youth and the bitterness she harbored against her family, especially her sister. In her twisted thoughts, Claudia had cheated her out of a happy childhood and teen years by robbing the attention of their parents.

She was not the old Abrielle anymore. She was not the Abrielle who was passed over by her parents, favoring Claudia. Her younger sister, at that! She was now Abrielle, Queen of the Order of Xander's Disciples! She now had everyone's attention. She was at the forefront. She had the power. She has indoctrinated the ability to control the destiny of any of the damned she chose outside of the ordSer. Success for such immense control consisted of a legion of steps that was the curriculum instilled into a select few within the order. She was one of those few. Abrielle set the process of such control into motion she mainly intended for Claudia.

* * * * * * * * * * * *

Avel Horan was the star of a weekly cable TV show, *Cults of Our Time.* He was scrolling the web for extremist sects and beliefs that would be interesting enough for his show. He was amused at sites about groups of *flat earthers* that balked at modern science, zealots that doubted the holocaust ever existed, eccentrics who believed the moon landing was a hoax, a far-right group who were brainwashed into believing that Donald Trump was the second coming of Christ, and other outlandish groups. These were such guests that made his show a success. He scrolled to a site about a woman who was the queen of the Order of

Xander's Disciples, a secret society that very little was known about.

The disciples have an actual queen now. Avel was amazed at the thought. *My viewers will go wild for this!* He had no luck reaching anyone at the cult's headquarters for an interview, but that was no surprise. He downloaded videos and pictures of the cult. However, only one of them included a purported image of the queen, through a dark website he planned to use for a fifteen-minute segment of his show. He was unable to find more pictures of their queen. Horan was fascinated by the story of the Xander order, but little was revealed. He was puzzled that more wasn't known about it, but as he dug deeper in his research, he discovered the sect keeps everything within the Xander family. Its members were forbidden to share anything with the outside world. When one of its former disciples publicly revealed too much of the affairs of the cult, she mysteriously died in an accident.

Claudia was in her first trimester and was due for an ultrasound. She had dialed her phone to make a doctor's appointment and was on hold while she listened to an annoying automated voice apologizing for the long wait time. She reached for the TV to turn down the volume when she caught a glimpse of a woman who had a striking resemblance to her sister on the *Cults of Our Time* show. It changed to a commercial before

Claudia could get a good look at the woman. When the show returned, it had moved on to another story. She thought nothing more about it and turned off the TV.

That evening she complained to Brent that she was having heavy abdominal cramping. When the pain persisted, he drove her to the emergency room where she had miscarried.

Brent stayed home from work the morning after to care for Claudia, who was exhausted from a sleepless night of crying from depression and just wanted to lay in bed. "Just let me lie here for a while," Claudia moaned.

The miscarriage was emotionally devastating for Claudia, as well as Brent. Regardless of his frustration and sadness, he remained strong for her after trying for more than two years to conceive.

"There must be something wrong with me for this to happen," said Claudia.

"There's nothing wrong with you. It's not your fault. It's nobody's fault. You're not alone. I'm devastated about this too. We'll get through this. We'll keep trying."

CHAPTER SEVEN

Austin Peters had always been exceptionally good with numbers and analysis. Therefore, he naturally became an IRS agent. He loved rubbing elbows with US attorneys, inspection generals, the FBI, agents for the Department of Homeland Security, and sometimes, US Marshals. Nothing gave him a rush like giving a courtroom testimony involving financial misconduct, for he loved the attention. Austin had conducted his fair share of investigations involving money laundering, financial fraud, embezzlement, and many other financial crimes. Off duty, when he had too much to drink in a bar, he would sometimes refer to himself as a *forensic accountant* and chasing the money trail.

He had aided in investigations that solved many small-time tax-evading cases, but that was his job. Within the service, he was a small fish in a vast pond. Unfortunately, Austin had only assisted in bringing down big businesses that cheated, but not never solely on his own. It was always others, who were more involved, that received praise from his superiors. Austin hardly received honorable mention in any of the significant cases.

He was getting close to the mandatory retirement age. He wanted to have just one big case of his own. He wanted one that would attract the attention of his superiors and the media across the nation.

Austin was studying an impressive tax return, but it would have seemed entirely normal if not for his keenly sharp eye. The name on the form was the *Order of Xander's Disciples.* After some inconsistencies in the calculations, he checked the back taxes for several years, and what he found had raised a red flag. Over time, the applicant seemed to have claimed too many charitable donations, reported too many losses on a Schedule C, and deducted too many business expenses. It was into the millions. He had many questions for this business and scheduled an audit. He stealthily bypassed the IRS's procedures so he could conduct it without getting others involved. Nicholas Xander owned the questionable business, and its finances stunk to high heaven. Austin yearned to bring Xander to justice and grab all the glory for himself.

He wrote to Xander's address, on record, for an appointment, including a questionnaire. He received a quick response by phone from an "associate" to schedule an appointment as he requested in his letter. Before the meeting, the questionnaire was quickly returned to him by mail with all of the questions answered and explained very satisfactorily and in detail. However, something didn't seem legitimate. There were some odd but clever discrepancies.

Xander's business address was more like a stately mansion. Austin received a warm welcome from a staff member on the morning of the appointment. He was led to the conference room by a man built like *Andre the Giant* and had a face that eerily reminded Austin of *Jabba the Hut*. He introduced himself as *Bruno,* who was Nicholas's bodyguard.

Several *staff* members were seated in the conference room, and all stood when Austin entered. One by one, each shook his hand and introduced themselves. Austin spent the day grinding through bank statements, documents, records, etc. He said he would present his report at a later date. Each member remained stoic until he left the room.

He admired the mansion once more as he looked back while driving away. He drove several miles down the freeway and his car that was in cruise control, began to accelerate. He tapped the brake to release it but kept going faster. He was up to almost a hundred miles per hour when he lost control and ran off the highway. He stirred the car through a thicket that slowed him down until it slammed into a shallow pond. He was able to jump out before the car began spinning in circles in the water because the engine was running at full speed. Austin was shaken but thankful to be alive, and he immediately suspected his automobile was tampered with. He knew someone tried to kill him and had little doubt who it could be. In his business, he had enemies but none who would want him dead. Nicholas Xander had a lot to lose due to the audit, including his freedom. Austin had deep reservations for not following protocol in the investigation. When Nicholas discovered that Austin had survived, he knew he was doomed.

* * * * * * * * * * * *

Abrielle was in her domain after another day of formal duties. She was provided with the very best of all the provisions when needed. Her meals were brought to her when there were no formal dinners but no snacks. She had to maintain a perfect figure to always be photogenic for the photo sessions. She was provided with the best cosmetics to keep her beautiful and even had extensive cosmetic surgery to enhance her looks. She had access to a doctor, dentist, and a hairdresser, too. All were dedicated disciples of the order. They all came to her wing when she was not busy participating in the sect's rallies.

She was at the top of the Xander empire, but Abrielle was denied some freedoms. She was prohibited from going anywhere, outside the property, without an escort. There was no television or radio anywhere at the headquarters. She was denied a computer and even a phone. She was conditioned not to need or want such luxuries during her years at the compound.

When her assistant retired, for the evening, to her quarters, she absently left her smartphone on the desk. The sight of the phone aroused Abrielle's curiosity. She touched it, and the screen lit up, displaying several social media icons. She pressed one, and the assistant's profile appeared on the website. A browser was at the top with an invitation to type in anyone's name or subject matter. She stared at the browser momentarily. Her prior conditioning subconsciously caused her to resist touching the keys. She forced herself to type in the first name that she thought of.

The profile image of Claudia popped up on the screen, and the memories of her caused Abrielle to shiver. Her heart was beating rapidly as she studied her sister's facial features. It took her a moment to find the button to scroll the website down. She fought back tears when she saw an old family picture of her and Claudia, as children, along with their parents. She scrolled down further to a written expression of sadness. It read *I'm sorry for your loss. Several other similar sentiments followed.* A post from Claudia replied with a thank you for the sentiments. She expressed sorrow for her *miscarriage* and how she and Brent were heartbroken but would get through their ordeal.

Miscarriage? Abrielle thought about the word and trembled for a moment with self-loathing for not feeling sadness over her sister's misfortune. On the contrary, she was happy over the loss. She smiled with self-satisfaction at Claudia's misery in retribution for her unhappiness caused by her sister. She was convinced her extraordinary powers were real, and her faith in her abilities was reinforced.

CHAPTER EIGHT

Austin gave a complete statement to the FBI and submitted all incriminating evidence against Xanders. Eventually, Austin was formally recognized for his brilliant work uncovering a monumental tax scheme. Afterward, he was surreptitiously forced to retire for failing to communicate the evidence earlier in compliance to the agency's procedure.

Nichola's operation had flourished without detection for two decades until one man, one virtuoso, who could see the encrypted fraudulence of its accounting procedures, that didn't seem possible. The same man had miraculously survived a car crash that should have killed him. While Austin was conducting the audit, Bruno had installed a device designed to cause Austin's car to lose control. The FBI had frozen all of Nichola's bank accounts, raided all of his properties, and arrested a long list of suspected accomplices.

The staff inside the Xanders's headquarters scrambled to destroy incriminating documents after receiving a tip that it would soon be raided. For the first time since she arrived, Abrielle was without any help. Her assistant was not in her quarters. When she stepped outside her suite, people were running in disarray. They ignored her, and she didn't know what was happening. Everyone in the Xanders family had always bowed to her and wouldn't dare disregard her. Finally, Christopher, a staff member, warned her that she was no longer safe and would have to get away before the FBI arrived. Abrielle felt helpless. It had been years since she had done anything without assistance. She commanded Christopher to help her, but he kept walking. When Abrielle changed her tone and started to plead with him, he stopped and turned back. "Follow me, quickly!"

"I must get my things first," Abrielle replied.

"There's no time! You either follow me right now or stay!" Christopher shouted.

"Where are we going?" Abrielle was stunned that anyone would have the audacity to yell at her, but she followed.

"We're going to the garage. Try to keep up."

Once they were in the garage, Christopher grabbed some car keys hanging on the wall. "Here's the keys to the *Ford Escort*."

"Why don't you drive?" Abrielle asked.

"I'm taking the *Lincoln*."

"It's been so long since I've driven. I don't have a license. Why can't I go with you?"

"I can't help you. You're not going with me. You're on your own!"

"I don't have any money!" Abrielle was crying.

Christopher reached for his wallet, gave her $200, got into the Lincoln, and sped away.

Her hands were shaky as she inserted the key into the ignition. She took a moment staring at all the controls. She had little confidence in her ability to drive, for it was many years since she was behind a steering column. She felt overwhelmed and tried to calm her nerves. She turned the ignition, and the engine came to life along with ear-piercing music from the radio. She fidgeted with various knobs until she found the volume control. Her heart raced when she slipped the gear shift to *drive* position. She had trouble, at first, controlling the accelerator and the vehicle's front, bobbing up and down. Once she made it to the street, she adjusted to the car's mobility. As she got further down the highway, she saw what appeared to be government cars sped by her and going in the opposite direction. Abrielle was driving aimlessly until she saw a road sign titled *Detroit 250 miles*. It was once her home.

* * * * * * * * * * *

Nicholas was on the run and hiding in a chateau that he provided for Elizabeth, one of his *kept women.* It was the last of his properties that authorities had not yet confiscated. Elizabeth was very aware that his empire had collapsed, and she was pondering her next step. Nicholas brooded as he sat in a recliner in the dark. He was thinking about his past, present, and future. He thought about death and dying. He didn't fear death, but it was the thought of dying. He was afraid of the last moments. His depression was paralyzing him. His mind was racing. He saw suicide as a solution.

Elizabeth was concerned and asked him what he was thinking and feeling, but he waved her away. She did as he asked, left the room, and closed the door. After two hours, she was getting worried. She stood outside the room and listened closely, but there was total silence. She knocked, but there was no response. She eased the door open and screamed at the sight of Nicholas hanging from a ceiling light.

CHAPTER NINE

When Randy Rudolph quit high school, he was under the illusion he would soon have a great job, a cool car, and live the life of a hard-partying, ladies' man. Nonetheless,is first job was doing back-breaking labor on a rock quarry. He was fired the first month after calling off sick, repeatedly. He had similar issues with the various jobs that followed. He didn't seem to fit anywhere. Six years later, he was between jobs, again. He still lived at home with his mother, who nagged him almost daily. He would take off each day, in his worn *Toyota,* just to get away from her. However, riding around in the community and killing time helped him discover a money-making opportunity. One morning, after snowing all night heavily, Randy's mother's sharp tongue was extra harsh. He wasn't planning to go out that day because of the weather, but he couldn't stand his mother nagging him another moment. He grabbed his keys, jumped in the car, and drove aimlessly. He was only a short distance away when he approached a vehicle stalled in the snow that blocked the street. Randy stopped, got behind the stalled car, and pushed it clear of the snow. The driver got out and thanked him profusely and gave Randy a twenty-dollar bill for his help. Elated by his good fortune, Randy decided to stop at a package store for some celebratory beer. A driver slid into Randy's car just as he got out at the store's parking lot. The only damage to Randy's car was a small dent. The driver of the other car was very apologetic and suggested they not get the insurance companies or the police involved. He offered Randy a hundred dollars in cash as a settlement.

Randy stood in the parking lot and stared at the stash of money as the motorist drove away. *A light bulb came on inside his head,* and he found the answer to his money issues without going through the hassle of working for it. Randy thought his *ship had finally come in.* He had found his niche. He would drive around and help motorist push their cars when stuck in the snow and give them a ride if they had car trouble, if it wasn't too far. The drivers almost always offer to pay him for being a good samaritan. If they didn't offer then he would ask for pay. Occasionally he would hit pay dirt. When it snowed heavily, as it often did, he would park so that it would make it improbable for other cars not to slide into his. He would always be a good sport about the accident and offer to take a cash settlement and spare the inconvenience of dealing with cops. He discovered the most straightforward way to make a buck is to purposely slam on his brakes, which would sometimes cause drivers, who follow too closely, to rear-end his car.

Abrielle had driven for hours before taking a wrong turn and was on a blacktop road. She thought she was lost but discovered she was approaching the outskirts of Detroit. Once there, she had no clue what to do next. The Ford Escort she was driving began to sputter. The brakes felt heavy, and she had to press hard to slow down. The steering wheel felt stiff, and she had to hold it tighter to keep the car under control. The engine had shut off, but she managed to pull off the highway and stop the vehicle. She turned the ignition key repeatedly, but the car wouldn't start for it was out of gas.

She looked out the window at her surroundings. All she saw were commercial buildings that were sparsely spaced, and there were no people around. It was getting dark. There were no other cars on the highway. She got out of the car and waited for a driver to pass that would be willing to stop and help. A car approached and slowed down as Abrielle tried to wave it over, but the driver didn't stop. It was several minutes before another car appeared.

Randy had drunk his last beer and was enjoying a good buzz. He wanted more, but he was broke. He was on his way home when he saw Abrielle's car on the side of the road. When eased closer, she waved at him to stop. He hoped she might only have a flat tire or some other minor problem. He would take care of it, put her back on the road and get a cash reward.

"Thank you for stopping," Abrielle said anxiously. "Please, can you help me? My car won't start." She assumed the authorities were looking for her, and she was afraid since she could only see his headlights. She feared he may have been a cop. She was relieved, judging by his appearance and considering the looks of his car.

"Yes, ma'am! I'll be delighted! I'll take a look. Do you mind if I try to start it?"

Randy got in the driver's seat. He immediately saw the stash of cash, sitting on the passenger side seat, that Christopher had given Abrielle during their escape from the headquarters. He turned the ignition switch to the *on* position but didn't detect any signs of engine problems on the display area. Then he noticed the gas gauge was empty.

"You're out of gas, ma'am," he announced while he was still seated in the car.

"No gas? Oh my!" Abrielle moaned embarrassingly.

"No problem! I can take care of it." The cash was stacked on the seat next to him, and he was wondering how much was there. "A gas station is just up the road a bit. Why don't you wait here and guard your car while I dash over to the station and bring back a container of gas? I can be back in a jiffy!"

"Why don't I go with you? The car will be ok."

Randy thought for a moment. He wasn't expecting that response. "No, really! You should stay here. I'll not be gone long."

"How are you going to bring the gas back here?

Again, Randy had to think for a moment. "Oh, I know the attendant at the gas station. He has lots of gas cans. I'll just grab one. No problem. You wait here." The dashboard and overhead lights had finally faded off, so it was dark enough for him to snatch all of the cash laying on the car seat.

Abrielle waited for over an hour. She desperately hoped that each car approaching would be Randy returning, but they came and went. She turned on the dashboard lights to check the time. She instantly saw that her money was gone. She cursed, then she cried. It was late, and the road was desolate. Exhausted and hungry, she maneuvered the back of the seat in a down position to rest and soon fell into a deep sleep.

CHAPTER TEN

In a dream, Abrielle aimlessly walked through the halls of a school. She was confused but somehow knew she had a class to attend, and she was late. She was worried about not having a textbook. She found the classroom and sat down but was unprepared for class. The teacher walked over with a paddle in her hand. She stared ominously at Abrielle. She repeatedly shouted something inaudible as she banged the ruler on Abrielle's desk.

The truck driver shined a flashlight through the driver's side window. The sight of Abrielle aroused him as she slept. He reached for the door handle to open, but it was locked. He tapped gently on the window so as not to startle her. There was no movement inside, so he knocked harder. She awakened with a jolt. She looked up at the glaring light and screeched when she saw the man outside the window.

"Relax! I'm just making sure you're alright." The truck driver tried to be reassuring as he shouted through the window.

"Who are you?" Abrielle was groggy from her sleep and was trying to focus. She readily noticed he was not the younger man she expected to return. She was naturally suspicious and was reluctant to open the car door.

"My name is Max. I was driving by and noticed your car. Do you need help?"

"I'm out of gas. I was waiting for another man, who had stopped earlier. He was to find a gas station not far from here. He didn't come back, and he took all the money that I had," Abrielle said urgently.

"Where are you headed?"

"Detroit."

"Well, you almost made it. Detroit is only a few miles away. He took your money and just left you here? Oh my! I'll tell you what. I don't think that guy is coming back. I'm almost home from my haul. There's nothing much we can do about your situation at this time of the morning. It's way past midnight. There are no service stations open. You better come along with me. You can stay with the missus and me tonight. We have a spare room with a small bathroom attached. We'll take care of your car issues later today after you've rested. I've been on the road all week, and I'm tired." He was still shining the flashlight through the window. Her dress was up past her knees and almost to her thighs. He tried not to stare at her bare legs.

Abrielle realized she had no choice. She got out of the car and followed Max to his semi-truck. He opened the passenger door and helped her in. She winced at his offensive body odor.

"Where is your home?" She asked.

"It's not far. We just need to get on the freeway and drive a short piece. The seats in these *Freightliners* are very comfortable, so relax. You must be exhausted. I'll call my wife and tell her we're coming. She'll prepare us a bite to eat. It's always a coming-home ritual. I'm often on the road for two weeks at a time. At the end of every trip, when I'm on the very last stretch, I call Elsie, no matter what time of day. She's always at the door to greet me. She gets lonely when I'm gone.

"I have no money to pay you for your help," Abrielle said.

Now, don't worry about that. You have enough to worry about. It's no problem to double back in the morning with a tank of gas to get your car running. You said that you were on your way to Detroit. Do you have people there?"

Abrielle's thoughts took her back to another life, so long ago, that she couldn't possibly return to. She remembered her decision to leave was not revocable.

Even if I could, then what? There's nothing for me there. So, why am I going back to Detroit?

"You feeling ok?" Max asked.

"Yes, just tired. I have personal business in Detroit. Are we almost there?"

"Not long. Just try to relax." Max glanced over at Abrielle and noticed she was dozing off. He pulled into a rest stop. She was snoring softly as he parked his rig. He reached into the console on the driver's side and pulled out a bottle of chloroform that he made in his basement. He placed it over her mouth and nose with a handkerchief. She took three deep breaths as she tried in vain to resist and then was out cold. He had become very skillful with the compound since he unintentionally killed a teenage runaway while administering it. He had to act quickly before she came around.

She awakened on a cot with a throbbing headache from the side effects of the chloroform. She was lying on her back, and adhesive tape covered her mouth. Her hands, as well as her feet, were tied. He warned her that if she screamed, he would gag her. He placed a bedpan under her and told her to use it or lie in her own waste. He left and returned later and removed the bedpan, and cleaned her. He left again and returned with food. He attempted to hand feed her, but she resisted. He told her to eat when he fed her or starve. After she finished her food, he said to her that he would untie her and she could get dressed. He warned her that if she gave him any problems, he would tie her up again. He went out again, and Abrielle began plotting her escape.

CHAPTER ELEVEN

A Michigan State Trooper ran the license plate on the Escort to see if it was stolen and to determine the ownership of the vehicle since it was abandoned. The plate number got the attention of the police dispatcher since it was under the name of Nicholas Xander. She immediately called the vehicle's location into the FBI's hotline as instructed for all police precincts in the nation that had any information about Nicholas Xanders. The FBI's evidence response team was in the area with the hour.

All law enforcement jurisdictions were in the pursuit but had few leads in their search and apprehension of Nicholas. With the discovery of the Escort that was in his name, the FBI remained hopeful for new information. The car was towed to be searched for clues.

Two FBI agents knocked on all the doors of residences in the vicinity, where the Escort stalled. Elsie Stemmer remembered the car vividly, for she saw Randy Rudolph in the driver's side, and his car was parked behind it. She typically wouldn't have given it any thought, but Elsie had a very low opinion of Randy. This was based on what she had heard about him from his mother. The two women talked sporadically at Tooties Salon, so Elsie didn't trust him. She was cooperative and helpful in giving the agents Randy's address and a thorough description of a woman standing next to the Escort. Elsie described the woman as well dressed, very beautiful, and high maintenance. The FBI had already rounded up all of Xander's Disciples' top brass except for Nicholas, the prime suspect, and the mysterious *Queen* Abrielle. The FBI knew very little about her and didn't even know if *Abrielle* was her real name. The agents were interested to know if the woman that Elsie described was the woman they were looking for. She was not a suspect in the money scheme or the attempted murder of Austin . However, the agents hoped that if they found Abrielle, she may know the whereabouts of Nicholas. The agent's next stop was at Randy's home. His mother was busy in the kitchen when she heard a knock on the front door. "I'll be right there!" She shouted. There was another knock and louder. "I said I'll be right there. Just keep your shirt on!" She opened the door and saw two agents in mundane dark suits. They oddly reminded her of actors in a *Men in Black* spoof.

"Mrs. Rudolph?" The taller agent asked.

"We don't need another vacuum cleaner or a set of encyclopedias." Beatrice snorted at her humor. "If you're Bible thumpers, you better get off my porch, now"!

"I'm special agent Jim Summers with the Federal Bureau of Investigation, and this is my colleague, special agent Mel Lance. We're looking for Mr. Randy Rudolph."

"Why? What do you want with Randy?" Beatrice asked.

"Oh, nothing to worry about. We just have a few questions."

Randy was in his bedroom and was awakened by the knock. He got up to investigate and went into the living room just as the agent announced they were the FBI. Startled, he turned to go back into his room. The agents were still standing on the front porch, and they both looked past Beatrice. "Are you Randy Rudolph?" Agent Summers asked.

Randy froze, and his heart was pounding. He had been a bundle of nerves ever since he agreed to stash a large shipment of stolen televisions and stereo equipment, for his cousin, in his mother's garage. He turned back around to face the front door. He tried to catch his breath as he struggled to answer. "Yeah." His response was barely audible.

"I'm special agent Jim Summers, with the Federal Bureau of Investigation, and this is special agent Lance.

Is it ok if we come in for a minute?" Beatrice opened the screened door for them to enter.

"What about?" Randy felt his bowels loosen.

"Relax, Mr. Rudolph. You're not in trouble or anything. We just have a few questions. It's not about you."

"Ok." Randy was breathing heavily, and he was terrified the men would ask to search his mother's garage.

"Thanks. Nice house."

"Yeah? Thanks." Randy tried to act naturally, but his mind was racing and trying not to panic.

"Did you see a blue Ford Escort parked by Shelby Road, the evening before last?"

The question about the car took Randy totally off guard, and he strained to think of a story to pass off on the agents concerning the $200 he stole. He got ahead of himself before he knew why the agents were asking about the circumstances that evening. "I had planned to give the money back," was all he could think to say.

"Yes, go on," agent Summers pressed him to elaborate. Neither agent was aware of the stolen money but could readily sense that it would be easy to make Randy tell everything he knew.

"I was just driving home and noticed a stalled car, so I decided to be a good Samaritan. I stopped to help. She was just out of gas. I was a little short on cash and just took the money lying on the seat to buy a gas tank down at Walter's filling station. I returned with the gas and the money, but she was gone. That's the way it happened."

"What was the woman's name?"

"She didn't say. I was only there a few moments, and then I was gone."

The agents quizzed Randy for a half-hour until satisfied they had all the information he had to offer. Randy sighed with relief as the agents turned to leave. Agent Summers looked back at Randy, gave him a stern glance, and warned him that someone would be in touch about the money he took.

A message was sent to all the agents assigned to search for Nicholas by the end of the day. The letter detailed that he was found dead of an apparent suicide. The hunt for the so-called, Queen of Xander's Disciples, had come to an end soon afterward. The FBI's only motive to search for her was that she may have had information about Nicholas's whereabouts. She had committed no known crimes. The authorities assumed she was only a girlfriend of Nicholas, and they had no information on her true identity.

CHAPTER TWELVE

There was only one small window, but it was tented, and Abrielle couldn't see through it. There were no clocks, so she lost all sense of time. The man who called himself *Max* came in and warned her not to attempt an escape. It seemed impossible, anyway. There was nothing in the small and confined room that could be used as a tool to break out. She could find nothing she could use as a weapon, and she could never overpower him, for he was too strong. His appearance repulsed her. He was morbidly overweight, and he stank as if he hadn't bathed in weeks. It was ironic, but he insisted that she bathe using a small shower each day. He told her to get used to him, for she would be his for a long time.

Despite his size, she was confident she could disable him if she kicked him in the groin and then jab her forefinger into his eye socket. This was part of her training, in martial arts, during the years she was at the compound. She was determined to fight him or die trying for that would be better than the living hell she was forced to endure. She had nothing to lose. She would wait behind the door and surprise him.

She heard the clicking sound of the key turning on the other side of the door. Her emotions were running high. Her heart began to flutter. Then it was as if it was leaping out of her chest. The door swung open. She turned the corner of the entryway and lunged. Her right foot landed hard and dead center between his legs, and he winced from the pain. She thrust her arm forward with the intent to jam her finger in his eye. He managed to block it and punched her with his closed fist that broke her nose. She fell backward and slammed her head on the floor that left her unconscious.

She was in agony when she awakened with her hands tied. Then, Abrielle heard a rumbling sound, the room was shaking, and it felt like it was moving. She had been in the sleeper of Max's truck all along. More hours had passed before the truck stopped. Max came in and warned her there was no escape, and if she tried again, he would kill her. He untied the ropes and left her a sack of *fast food*. It had always been such food since her abduction. He left, and soon afterward, the truck began to move again.

Abrielle's only clothes were the unwashed *Bodycon* dress she wore when abducted. Max brought Abrielle a pair of worn and ill-fitting floral pants from the eighties and an *Aerosmith* T-shirt. Max returned later, picked up her dress, and walked out with it. Gone with it were the last remaining remnants of her former life. She was terrified of the horrendous days to come.

It was when the roar of the rig's engine stopped that was the worst for her, for that meant Max would be back in the sleeper. She heard the sound of the sleeper's door, once again, unlocked. Once again, she shut her mind off the thought that he may try to rape her. He rushed toward her and raised a handkerchief to her face. Within seconds she passed out from the chloroform.

She awakened to the smell of cat feces and mildew. It was dark, but she knew she was no longer in the semi's sleeper and afraid to move. She remained still until she heard a door creak open and footsteps walking down a flight of stairs. A light came on that blinded her. Max was standing over her.

"Welcome to your new home! You'll like it here once you get used to it, but don't get too cozy. We're on vacation for two whole weeks! After being on the road constantly, I just like to lounge right here in the ole shack. Now, take everything off." Abrielle obeyed without resistance, for doing so could result in a belting on her bare bottom as done before. She was his property. He owned her as she was reminded, over and over. When he left the room, the light stayed on. She looked around. There was one window in the sleeper, but it was tented and covered with steel security bars. She assumed she was in a basement or was it a dungeon? The entrance door was at the top of the flight of stairs. The twin-sized bed was the only furnishing.

* * * * * * * * * * * *

It wasn't about sex with Max. It was about the power he had over Abrielle. *Darrell,* Max's real name, had always been obese since he was a child. His overbearing father caused Darrell to feel inadequate, and he developed low self-esteem.

He was the biggest kid throughout the school. His third-grade teacher, Mrs. Hamer, took all the students' weight for the school record. When Darrell stepped on the scales, Mrs. Hamer cried out, "Darrell, you're as big as a barrel!" The name, *Darrell Barrel,* stuck throughout his school years, and he was bullied unmercifully. Despite his size, he was unwilling to defend himself out of fear of his tormentors. They would stick his head in the toilet and flush it. They would slam metal garbage cans over his head and bang the sides. Because of his ample size, he would get stuck in the can as he staggered and fell to the ground while the other students would chant *Darrell Barrel.*

During a recess, Priscilla, a cheerleader, flirted with Darrell from a distance. She motioned for him to walk over to where she was standing. He thought she was the most beautiful girl in school and couldn't believe she had noticed him. She asked him if he would like to meet her at the football bleachers to talk privately. It was just after heavy rain, and he did as she asked. He waited at the bleachers for most of the recess, and he began to leave in frustration. Suddenly, he was body-slammed to the ground. Priscilla's boyfriend, Ralph, the quarterback for the school team and several other players, began kicking him as he wallowed in the mud. Just before blacking out, he looked up to see Priscilla laughing.

When he revived, Darrell was still lying in the mud. Recess was over, and he walked into his next class, muddy and late. His teacher demanded he tell her why he was so muddy, but he kept quiet. Then he was scorned by the teacher as his classmates laughed.

Later that day, Priscilla jeered and snickered as she walked past him in the hall. Something inside him snapped, and he beat her in an uncontrollable rage. The assault put Priscilla in the hospital and landed Darrell in the Michigan State Reform School.

Darrell's social skills never developed, and he had become hostile toward women. When he started running over-the-road truck hauls, he discovered that picking up naïve runaway teens was easy. He loved to humiliate them. He craved the power he had over them.

Allowing them to live was not an option. Eventually, he changed his name to Max.

* * * * * * * * * * *

Max spent much of his vacation time lounging and drinking large quantities of liquor. The more he drank, the more distorted his perversions became. He had been resisting his urge to bask in his ultimate thrill to torture Abrielle to death but slowly. The time had arrived as it had with all the others. He was overcome with excitement as he sat in his recliner.

The hours of isolation were excruciating and endless for Abrielle. No words could describe the sound of Max's footsteps as he came down the basement stairs. The door creaked open, and a terrible dread poured over her with each footstep. She looked in utter bewilderment as he lost his balance and fell forward. His feet slipped out from under him, and he plunged headfirst and slammed it against the concrete floor that sounded like a melon bursting. He momentarily shook violently and then lay motionlessly. Abrielle stared in confusion for several seconds. She was unsure of what had just happened. She thought he might have staged an accident to tease her. However, that wasn't it. He certainly wasn't teasing, for she saw blood forming around his head. She eased closer and saw no movement.

She detected no sign of breathing. She was convinced that it wasn't just a random accident but a direct result of her divine will. Her power had not left her.

She saw the door above the stairwell was ajar. The only way she could climb the stairs was to step over Max. She feared that he would somehow revive and grab her leg as she stepped over. *That's impossible, or is it? He's not moving or breathing, and there's a pool of his blood all over the floor. Could he, for some reason, be faking? Could this be a demented joke?*

Abrielle decided to wait no longer. She leaped over him quickly and raced up the steps. When she got to the top, she looked back and saw that Max still wasn't moving. She feared troubling possibilities that she hadn't considered. Could someone else be in the house who would stop her from escaping? Would the front door of the house be locked? She turned away from the basement entrance to face total darkness. She felt along the wall for a light switch but found none. She turned a corner, and light from the moon furnished some visibility. She eyed the front door of the home and walked toward it but tripped over a stool. She bumped her knee when she fell, but she got up and continued making her way to the front door. She was just a mere few feet away from freedom and the end to her misery at the hands of Max. She grabbed the door handle and turned the lock, but it still wouldn't open. She felt the surface over the knob and found the deadbolt. She turned it, opened the door, and darted out. It was dark, but the weather was warm. She was in an older neighborhood of small bungalows that stood close together. All the house lights were out, indicating it was probably early morning. She wasn't sure but she was almost positive she was in River Rouge and near the Detroit city line. She looked over the horizon and saw the city lights.

She estimated she was only about four miles from the downtown area She began walking in that direction and then stopped. She was worried that Max might not be dead, after all. She feared that he may recover and come after her, or was she just terror-stricken? She had to know for sure. She had to make sure he was dead. She walked back into the house and eased her way through the darkened living room. She stood perfectly still to listen to any movement. She saw an outline of a lamp, turned its switch on, and saw the entrance to what must be the kitchen just a few steps away. She slowly walked through the sink area, searched through the kitchen drawers, and grabbed a seven-inch cook's knife. She continued walking to the basement and looked down the stairwell to see Max still lying in the same position, face down. He had not moved, but that didn't matter. She walked down the steps while firmly clutching the kitchen knife. When she reached the bottom step, she stared at Max and thought about his control over her. The rapes and beatings raced through her mind. At that moment, it didn't matter if he was already dead. Overcome by uncontrollable rage, she stooped down and plunged the knife deeply and repeatedly for gratification and revenge.

* * * * * * * * * * * *

Abrielle was still wearing the same Aerosmith T-shirt and unshapely floral pants. She was hungry and penniless. She assumed she was a fugitive, so she didn't report her kidnapping to the authorities. She was exhausted when she reached Griswold Street in downtown Detroit after walking for almost four miles. It was still dark, and Abrielle went into a narrow alley between two buildings to hide and rest. The pavement was uncomfortable, and she could smell garbage overflowing from a nearby trash bin. None of this distracted her from the peace and serenity she oddly felt, for she was free from Max forever.

* * * * * * * * * * * *

Roberta hadn't heard from her brother, Max, in weeks. Upon driving to his house, she discovered his front door was ajar. As soon as she entered the living room, there was an overwhelming stench that she thought must have been a dead rodent. She called out for Max several times. She moved slowly from room to room and then down to the basement. When she found his body lying in a pool of blood, her screams could be heard from a block away.

Marlowe was proud to be a 911 police dispatcher and first responder in life and death emergencies. Often enough, during her twelve and sometimes sixteen-hour shifts, she received her share of nonemergency calls. People would call to report they're unable to remember where they parked their cars, theft of a license plate or bicycle, and noisy parties. She sometimes received calls asking about road conditions, disputes over rent payments, and other civil complaints. Such calls were an annoyance to Marlowe, but when she did receive calls that were legitimate emergencies, adrenaline would flow through her. Her skin would tingle, and she would swing into action. She had received a call from a hysterical woman, reporting that she found her brother dead in his basement.

The first respondent at the murder scene was police sergeant Wallace, who vomited at the sight of Max's mutilated body with so many stab wounds. Homicide detective Biggerstaff leaned over to inspect Max's body. His first thought was that the profile of the assailant must have held a deep-seated grudge for the victim.

He didn't want to unconsciously make assumptions before forensic specialists gathered evidence. Samples of blood, hair, and semen were collected for DNA that eventually revealed a positive match of at least five women. Over the span of ten years, these unsolved cold cases spread across the entire nation. One other DNA match involved a Ford Escort in the name of the notorious Nicholas Xander.

CHAPTER THIRTEEN

It was the beginning of another business day in Detroit. Professionals and other city dwellers hurriedly walked along the sidewalk. Noisy vehicles congested the streets that awakened Abrielle, lying on the alley's bare pavement and just a few yards off Griswold. The area was common for the homeless, who the regular business crowd and frequent shoppers mostly ignored. It was believed that giving handouts to beggars made the problem of vagrancy and panhandling worse. It was also illegal to hand out food or money. Therefore, few gave Abrielle a second glance when she ventured out of the alley. She had not eaten the past twenty-four hours, and she was desperate for food. Nearby, she could smell the aroma of donuts sold by a street vendor. She studied each passerby with the hope of finding someone who she thought would help her. She tried to think of a believable lie. It would have to be a plausible story that would tug at the heart.

A short, overweight, middle-aged man, who was well dressed, glanced at Abrielle as he walked by. "Sir, can you help me? I sat my shoulder bag on that bleacher over there. I turned to see if the bus was coming and when I turned back around, my bag was gone!" She said this as straightforwardly and honestly as she could. "It was just an old bag. Thank God there wasn't anything but a little money and makeup in it. The purse is no big loss, but I need bus fare. Could you possibly help me?"

The man studied her for a moment as she flashed him a suggestive smile. "Sure, I can help you," he answered as he reached into his hip pocket. He retrieved an expensive-looking wallet that reminded her of the one that Nicholas owned, and he opened it to reveal a large stash of bills.

She observed as he began to pull out a five-dollar bill. "Sir, I just need to get to my home in Romulus. It's so far out, and the fare is more expensive." She pretended to cry. He looked at her compassionately and pulled out a twenty.

She spent much of the day wandering the streets until a couple stopped her. They asked if she had anywhere to sleep for the night, and they directed her to a homeless shelter. Abrielle was embarrassed for how she was dressed, and she could see the pity in their eyes. She made her way to the shelter and walked inside. Its appearance reminded her of a doctor's clinic, for it was clean and sterile. However, it had the faint odor of a second-hand clothing store. Abrielle was given a registration form and a list of rules. When she completed the form and handed it back to the front desk, the attendant asked for her identification. Having none, she claimed she lost all her IDs and hadn't yet replaced them. Her bed would not be available until after dinner. She had to wait outside of the shelter with swarms of others for the evening meal at 7:00 p.m. Dinner was a choice of peanut butter and jelly or tuna sandwiches. Breakfast would be at 6:30 a.m., but afterward, she and the others would have to leave for the day. This was to encourage the residents to look for a job.

She was escorted to her sleeping area to a room the size of a walk-in closet that once housed her shoes. Its only furnishing was a single cot and a chair. An attendant came through and gave her and the others a towel to shower. During the evening, she got acquainted with the other female residents. Most had substance abuse issues, and others had been beaten by their partners. Some had just gotten down on their luck like Abrielle, except in her case, she was down on her luck to an extreme. Only a few women there fit the stereotype she had always imagined. She was thankful to lie down for the night without fear in many weeks.

* * * * * * * * * * *

She was feeling uneasy over the knock on the door. There was another knock and still another that continued until it escalated into a violent pounding. A sense of doom overcame her. There was no escape, and the pounding persisted. Who or what was behind the door as it began to creak open? The shelter's councilor rushed into Abrielle's quarters upon hearing her screams and shook her awake from her nightmare.

After a scrimpy breakfast of boiled eggs and toast, Abrielle and all the other residents were rushed out of the shelter for the day. She stood on the front steps brooding over her predicament, and it was difficult for her to conjecture. She started walking down the sidewalk with no plan for a solution. She stopped to look into a dress shop window to admire a *Valentino* gown and *Gucci h*andbag. She pondered when she had a wardrobe closet full of such clothing, along with jewelry drawers and vanities, that served as a badge of honor. She recoiled at the reflection of her appearance in the window. She was still wearing the Aerosmith T-shirt and floral pants. She strained to look at the image of her face, in the window, with no makeup and unkempt hair. Then she saw another reflection of a man behind her that caused her to freeze in terror. The man appeared to be Max standing at the bus stop, but she was too afraid to turn around. A city bus approached, and just as he climbed the bus steps, she turned around but saw he was not Max. Since her escape from him, she had been in shock and denial. After witnessing the reflection of the man, who she thought was Max, caused her to have a flashback that turned her stomach. She bent over and vomited in plain sight of people on the sidewalk. She collapsed on the pavement as a result of dizziness and despair.

"Drink this, honey." A woman held out a water bottle to Abrielle, as she struggled to sit up. It was difficult to guess the woman's age because of her rough and weathered complexion. "You think it may have been the eggs at the shelter that didn't agree with you?"

"I'm not sure," Abrielle replied. "Thank you for the water."

"My name is Clementina. I was at the next table over. The food is atrocious sometimes, but I shouldn't complain. It's better than nothing. Sip the water. You need to get something in your belly. I have an apple you should eat. It's a long time until dinner. Theyserve it at six-thirty, you know. They have fried chicken and potatoes tonight.

"Would you help me up, please? Everyone's staring."

Clementina grabbed Abrielle's upper arm. "You pay them no mind. You're not feeling well. They'll get over it. Now, the cops are another thing. You have to watch out for them. The shelter is no picnic, but the Detroit jail is one place where you don't want to spend the night! What's your name?"

Her mind took her back to when she was once called a queen, and thousands of disciples adulated her name. "I'm Abrielle."

"Abrielle! What a beautiful name," Clementina gushed. "It's good to meet you."

"Likewise," is all Abrielle could say.

"Well, we're going to be good friends. I'm curious to know your story. We all have one, you know."

'I'm sure." Abrielle looked around at her surroundings. "Tell me, Clementina, is there somewhere we can sit and get some coffee?"

"There sure is! That would be *Georgie's,* around the corner. It's a diner I go to when I can afford it. You should get yourself something to eat cause you're going to need your strength to get through the day. They have a decent breakfast menu, and it's a great place to get off our feet."

"I'll buy." Abrielle still had most of the cash the well-dressed man gave her the day before.

"Not necessary, but thanks for the offer anyway. Bless your heart. Just follow me."

They entered the diner and sat in a booth next to a window. "I think I'll order the fruit salad and coffee," Abrielle mulled over the menu.

"Just coffee for me," said Clementina. I had a big breakfast at the shelter. I had two boiled eggs, and I hid the third one in my pouch. We're not supposed to take extras, but I'm careful not to get caught. They're strict about that. I'd hate to get the boot from the shelter. I have nowhere else to go. How about you, Abrielle?"

She considered the question, but she wasn't ready to go into details about herself. "It's not much to tell. Perhaps, I'll share more about myself later. You said you have nowhere else to go besides the shelter? Why is that, if I may ask?"

"I became an orphan when I was about seven years old. I remember my Daddy hitting me. I recall crying a lot, and I was always hungry. They came and got me and took me away to live in an orphanage. I remember I was scared because some of the bigger girls picked on me, but I got used to it. When I was ten, a family took me in. I was with them for a couple of years. They didn't hit me, but Ingrid, my foster mother, began resenting me for whatever reason, so I ran away when I was twelve. When the police found me, they sent me back to that same orphanage. For a long time, I didn't think I would ever have a fair shake in life, but when I think about that now, I know much of it was my own doing."

"Oh my!" Exclaimed, Abrielle. "It doesn't sound like any of it was your fault."

"You're very kind, Abrielle. I meet a guy while still in the orphanage. I was sixteen, and I ran away to marry him. He would hit me as my real Daddy did. I don't know why I put up with it for so long, but I finally left him after ten years of marriage. I've been off the street ever since."

"So, you're about twenty-six, now?" Asked Abrielle. She guessed Clementina to be about forty.

"I'm twenty-eight. I've been living in the shelter for the past three months. It's a lot better than sleeping in a cardboard box or on a bench like before. Was last night your first time at the shelter?"

"You said it will be serving chicken this evening?" Abrielle tried to divert the subject away from her issues.

"They sure are, and it's not bad. It's deep-fried, and they normally serve mashed potatoes. I hope you're coming back tonight. You'll get used to the shelter. Tomorrow is Thursday, and that's when the mission brings in a big box of clothes to give the residents. I'm not picky. I just take whatever fits, but sometimes there are some high-class blouses, pants, and even shoes that's hardly been worn! I can't figure out why folks don't want them. Rich people donated all the clothes, you know."

"We'll have to check it out." Abrielle wasn't listening. She was overcome by depression and anxiety due to the ordeal with Max. She would need a friend to help pass the time during the long daytime hours and on the street away from the shelter. Clementina was the only one she had. "So, what's next? I mean, what do you do all day before you go back to the shelter?"

"I go to the park that's not far from here. We can rest there and get off our feet. It has plenty of bleachers. The cops never bother me unless I'm still there after it closes. They have bathrooms there too. There's a hotdog vendor at the park on Saturday. It sells other things too, like chips and candy bars. Going to the park is better than standing on the street all day. There's no good way to use the bathroom or get off your feet on the avenue. There's so much walking to get anywhere. It wears me out, but there are things to do if you don't mind walking. The Presbyterian church gives away food on Fridays, but it's two miles away. That means two miles back. We better leave before the manager gives us the eye for sitting here too long. A lot of us, from the shelter, come here, and he doesn't like us."

"Good idea." Abrielle didn't want to draw attention. "Why don't we check out that park." They exited the diner, and Abrielle tried not to allow her anxiety to overpower her. She feared she could be recognized by any masses walking along the sidewalk. Many seem to stare directly at her. She jumped at the sound of a car horn only a few yards away.

"It's ok, Abrielle! I promise not to let anything happen to you", assured Clementina. "Take my arm, and we'll cross the street together when the light turns green."

They made it to the park, away from the city noise. Abrielle sat on a bleacher and enjoyed the trees and flowers. She realized the beauty of bird sounds that echoed in her ears for the first time. She looked up at the clouds that reminded her of a young girl. She remembered when she would lie on her back and look up to the sky. She would daydream about how life would be as a grown-up. She thought about her sister and parents, who thrived on providing her all the opportunities.

"Hey, Abrielle!" Said Clementina with a laugh. "You seem to be in another world. You sure you're ok?"

"I'm good. Thank you for bringing me here. It's very peaceful." Abrielle escaped into her thoughts again and wondered how long she would be in her predicament. She knew she must find a plan to dig her way out.

CHAPTER FOURTEEN

Detective Hunter's retirement was forthcoming, but the unsolved missing person case on Abrielle Kanazawa, would haunt him indefinitely. The family insisted he keep the search active, years after Abrielle's trail had gone cold. There was little background information on her, including a nonexistent employment record. She had no history of bank or credit card accounts and no jail record. Not even a single traffic ticket. Her driver's license hadn't been renewed since her disappearance.It was apparent that she was deceased. Hunter checked out every possible longshot over the twenty years since she was last seen.

Hunter scrolled through Abrielle's file that he had accumulated through the years. He began to search for anything he could have missed. He had previously studied hundreds of women's images with the name *Abrielle*, or similar in looks. He decided to download some updated files, and with modern technology, he was able to transfer some complete profiles instead of names and photos only. A few had similar physical characteristics, but none were whom he was looking for. He also used facial recognition software to run available photos of Abrielle through its database, and he got one match.

He studied the image in the cryptic Xander's Disciples photo he downloaded from the *Cults of Our Time,* TV show's website. However, he suspected it was a glitch in the software. The picture had some resemblance to Abrielle, but it seemed impossible for both to be the same person. Hunter thought It was unimaginable for a girl who grew up in a typical suburban middle-class family could rise to such heights in a notorious but otherwise, little-known occult. He spent hours searching the web for more images of the woman but found none. *Such a highly secretive sect,* he thought. Hunter marveled at the lengths it made to keep its activities *under the radar.* After digging deeper, he found dozens of members closely associated with the so-called *disciple*s. He gathered data on all former members he could find who may know their purported queen.

The detective was tempted to check with Abrielle's family about the facial matches. Considering multiple false alarms with a lookalike, Jane Does' and the living who had the same name, he decided to hold back over the years. He first wanted to contact the queen's fellow members in Xander's hierarchy, who would be willing to talk. Most had fled or were incarcerated, pending trial for their part in the tax fraud. They were a longshot, but they were the only leads. He gained access to a list of addresses of the members who were free on bond. He would visit them first before interviewing the others, where they were held without bond at the correctional institutions. Encountering such people as these were the most interesting part of his work.

The first former Xander member that Hunter visited was Felicia Montana, held in the Detroit Detention Center. On his arrival, Hunter had his visiting order checked by the staff and then a pat-down search just like any other visitor. He then made his way to the visit hall, where Felicia was seated. She was once a certified public accountant in a prominent finance firm but was entangled by the allure of Xander's cult. She allowed its wonder and delight to exploit her like many other professionals. She abandoned the firm to dedicate her life to the Xander faith. She was manipulated to believe the disciples were above the accountants' ethical code of conduct, which she swore to uphold. The disciples had such control over her mind that she thought that each fraudulent tax misdeed was good as long as it benefited the Xander family, financially. She was enthralled by Xander's brilliantly foolproof tax system that could never be detected. A noticeably beautiful lady, Felicia looked out of place in her oversized orange and white strip garb.

"All that I know about our queen is that she was sent to us by God," Felicia declared. "That's all I can and will tell you, Mr. Hunter.

Is the girl in this photo your queen?" Hunter presented the last known picture of Abrielle before her disappearance.

Felicia twitched when she looked at the image. "I have nothing more to say to you," and she looked away.

Hunter had no doubt she recognized the picture, but she refused to answer any more questions. "Your queen has been missing and maybe dead." He wasn't sure of this but wanted to get Felicia's reaction.

"Queen Abrielle will return in her absolute glory and free me of this loathsome place!"

"How do you expect her to do that?"

"She will free me through divine intervention, you fool!"

"Don't count on it," Hunter said as he turned and walked away. Hunter wondered if Felicia was aware of Abrielle's whereabouts and expected her to make bail. He informed the detentions' staff of this possibility, although it was unlikely.

Lars De Luca had lofty ambitions within the Xander hierarchy. He had only risen to the equivalency of a custodian but felt destined to be part of the upper echelon. He was Nicholas's first cousin, who rescued Lars from a psychiatric hospital. He was confined there after parading in the nude inside an upscale mall in Troy, Michigan. Lars was released in Nicholas's care, which he swore an oath of loyalty. He has had a history of psychotic behavior since he was young. As a teenager, he cared little about his appearance and hygiene. He began to hear voices at night that told him that he would one day have superpowers. He had been in and out of mental facilities his entire life. Now that Nicholas was dead, Lars felt it was his destiny to reign over the Xander family. In Lars's distorted mind, it was his rightful place and duty. He was unconcerned that he was forced to exist in a cramped doss house after fleeing the Xander headquarters stolen by its persecutors. However, he believed it was a mere setback. Lars had the unshakable belief that he was the new Xander messiah. He thought that was what the voices meant by *superpowers*. Nicholas was its messiah before him, but he was gone. Lars had been waiting months for a sign from God to begin his reign. He believed he had received it when a stranger showed him a picture of Queen Abrielle. Lars thought the stranger was actually an angel but disguised as a detective? *God certainly works in mysterious ways,* he thought. *The angel searched for the queen, but she hid from the persecutors. God sent the angel to me to help find her.*

CHAPTER FIFTEEN

Hackett had been a professional chef in some of the best restaurants of Detroit during his heyday. He had met some of the most prominent people in the city, including Lee Iacocca, the auto industry titan. Unfortunately, excessive alcohol consumption was Hackett's downfall. His drinking problem resulted in losing job after job and his reputation. He ultimately became homeless and was living at the shelter. During the evenings, he would help in the kitchen with the grand illusion that he would one day become a great chef, once again. He was attending AA meetings at the shelter and applied for several restaurant positions thanks to the help of office staff. With each rejection, the urge to drink grew. One job application forwarded to a restaurant near the shelter looked promising. It was a job washing dishes, but he scoffed at the opportunity. The shelter's counselor advised him not to be choosy and take the job if offered. However, it was another rejection that frustrated Hackett. His craving for a drink pulled at him and harder this time.

Hackett walked over to Wally's Bar n' Grill on the street corner from the shelter. He studied the bottle of his favorite bourbon on the shelf across from the bar. *Just one drink,* he thought. The bartender poured him a shot. He sipped it slowly, and it was going down nicely. So smooth that he decided to have another and a few more after that.

He struggled to maintain as he walked back to the shelter. His kitchen duties for that night were to fry frozen potatoes. He poured the oil into the large vat, and while it heated, he decided to take a quick bathroom break that took longer than he planned. The oil began to burn, and smoke filled the room. Marianne, a kitchen assistant, panicked and poured a pan of water over it, causing the oil to explode. The wall behind the stove began blazing with fire that triggered the alarm. Fortunately, all the residents and staff escaped the building, but the shelter was destroyed.

* * * * * * * * * * *

Abrielle and Clementina spent the daylight hours picking up empty beverage containers. They sold the cans and bottles back to grocery stores for ten cents each. That was a policy in Michigan, and they had collected a decent haul for the day. Clementina enjoyed spending the money on sweet snacks and other treats that weren't usually available at the shelter. Realizing that cashing in bottles and cans would take far too long to save, Abrielle looked for other means of income. She began shoveling snow from sidewalks in storefronts and window cleaning to help make extra income.

They took their bounty of bottles and cans for cash exchange at a supermarket and were hurrying back to the shelter before dinner. Black smoke filled the air as they walked closer, but parking cones blocked the street. Firetrucks, ambulances, and police cruisers swarmed the area as Abrielle looked in horror at her shelter in flames. She and Clementina's few possessions, such as clothes, were destroyed. All of the residents were forced to find other means of assistance. Some area churches provided temporary, emergency accommodations, including soup kitchens. Due to the overflow of the shelter's former residents, the provisions the churches struggled to offer were not enough to handle the hordes of displaced people. The long walk to the soup kitchens, waiting in long lines, and returning to these areas, where vagrancy was heavily enforced, was grueling for Abrielle. The only makeshift shanties and homeless camps that weren't aggressively prohibited lined the backstreets near the ruined shelter.

ABRIELLE

Abrielle was faced with the harsh reality of living permanently on the streets. From the beginning, Clementina, who had more experience with survival, promised to protect her and never leave her alone. She remained loyal to Abrielle for months that ultimately would turn into years. Abrielle's life and her chance to return to normalcy were long gone. To make her plight even worse, she had discovered cocaine. At first, she had resisted it but was told it would help her forget all her troubles. Contrary to a girl who set out to trample underfoot, everyone to prevail, Abrielle's confidence was virtually zero.

CHAPTER SIXTEEN

Detective Hunter departed the flophouse that sheltered Lars De Luca and thought he was one of the strangest people he had ever interviewed. He was astonished that De Luca, a grown man who lived in squalor, could be so delusional to believe that Hunter was an angel sent by God just because he presented a picture of Abrielle. Nonetheless, De Luca gave the response that Hunter was hoping for, for he made a positive match. Abrielle Kanazawa was the same person as the woman, the Order of Xander's Disciples, hailed as its queen. However, when pressed for more information about the queen, it triggered a seemingly bipolar episode for De Luca became nervous and started shouting incoherently. He wasn't venting at Hunter directly but as if he was angry at an imaginary person in the room. When Hunter returned to his office, he called his client, Wilder Kanazawa, with the news about his daughter.

"I don't believe it," proclaimed Wilder when he and Bethany met with Hunter. "This picture resembles my daughter, but what proof do you have that it's her and that she is a cult leader? Give me a break!"

"I believe it's more of a ceremonial position in the Xander order to give it legitimacy, from what I know," explained Hunter. "The proof was revealed through identification by one of the order's former members and by a facial recognition database. There's strong evidence that the *queen* is your daughter. The bad news is that she's been missing for months after the Xander headquarters was raided."

"So, Abrielle has been alive and well after all these years! Oh, thank God!" Bethany said excitedly.

"We know she was certainly alive last year, considering the last photo I've found. The FBI raided the cults' main facility, where Abrielle lived."

"She must have escaped and is hiding from those people," Wilder presumed.

"…or from the authorities, but I've checked it out, and there are no charges filed against her. She's not even considered a person of interest," Hunter added. "The Fed's don't know who she really is. They would like to question her, but it's not high on their list of priorities. Most of those who were part of the tax scheme had been found. They're hoping she may cooperate as a witness in court."

* * * * * * * * * * * *

Lars stepped out of his ramshackle dwelling with the fantasy that he would finally live the life he had imagined. "The queen and I will soon reign over our disciples!" He shouted aloud with delight. The other residents paid little attention, for they were used to his hysterics.

Lars was aware of Nichola's suicide but was convinced It was Gods' will and by His hand. He thought the all-mighty used Nicholas as a tool to pave the way for Lars to lead the Xander's Disciples to become its new messiah. It had been planned since his youth when he heard the voice's he presumed were messages from above.

CHAPTER SEVENTEEN

Clementina's breathing ability became increasingly labored, and she complained of muscle pain throughout her body. Abrielle feared her friend was infected with a virus sweeping the country. Fortunately, the two were currently staying in refugee housing. The caseworkers moved Clementina to a cramped, private quarter, away from the other residents until a nurse could come in to administer a test. Although limited, public funding allowed health care personnel to make rounds when possible and was often scarce. More residents showed similar symptoms, so a medical doctor came in and took all sick to area hospitals, but it was too late for Clementina. Abrielle would visit her daily but remain outside a partition as a precaution. They couldn't visibly see each other, but they could talk. Clementina seemed to be feeling better, and Abrielle was relieved. On her last visit, Abrielle assured her that medical care would arrive, and they talked about how they would soon leave the shelter and begin living everyday life. Late that night, Abrielle was awakened by some commotion, so she got up to witness Clementina being placed on a stretcher to be transported to the morgue.

Most deceased are surrounded by loved ones and memorialized at a service, but that wasn't the case for Clementina. She was held at the Wayne County Medical Examiner's office until a funeral Director agreed to take her body and attempted to locate her next of kin. After none were found, the state eventually cremated her.

* * * * * * * * * * * *

Claudia placed her cell on her desk after speaking with both her parents. She was stunned at their news about Abrielle and the possibility that she was alive and may soon be found. She started to call her husband when her secretary came in to inform her that a client was waiting in the lobby. Claudia switched her mind to business at hand. After a long day at her law office, she called Brent with the news, who was away for the week on business. When Claudia arrived home, she went through the motions to make herself a meal and prepare for sleep. She laid in her bed for hours, still trying to digest the news. She began wondering what her sister had been doing all those years. Although much time had been lost, she was overjoyed with anticipation at the possibility there still may be a chance that Abrielle would be found safe and be part of the family, once again. Overcome with emotion; she kneeled at her bedside to give thanks.

* * * * * * * * * * * *

Lars sat with his back leaning against a building at his usual spot. His hat lay on the sidewalk next to him to allow pedestrians the opportunity to put money in it. To him, they were all just part of the masses. They were the *damned*. He studied the phone number and address on the card that Hunter handed to him. "Contact me if you have any information. That was the angel's exact words!" Lars shouted out loud as people walked along the opposite end of the sidewalk to avoid him. On their way to lunch, two accountants walking by looked at Lars in disdain. He looked back at them with a scowl. Their opinions of Lars didn't matter to him. "They are all fools", he shouted to no one. "They don't realize who I am. They don't understand, but they will very soon. Very soon, indeed!"

He continued staring at the card and negative thoughts about the visitor. Lars wondered if the angel was an imposter. Rage was taking over as he was convinced the visitor could have been a soldier for the persecutors trying to destroy the Xander disciples. Lars rose from the sidewalk and began walking. His destination was the address on detective Hunter's business card.

CHAPTER EIGHTEEN

Ingrid was curious by the strange man's odd behavior, but she managed a pleasant greeting and flashed a fake smile. "How may I help you?"

"I was given this." Lars handed the secretary, Hunter's business card. She took the card and handed it back.

"You would like to see Detective Hunter?"

"Yes! Detective Hunter. Is he here?"

"I'll see if he's available. Your name, please?"

"Lars De Luca."

"Do you have an appointment?"

"No appointment. He told me to let him know if I needed to talk."

"I see, Mr. De Luca. Why don't you have a seat."

Ingrid got up from behind her desk and knocked on Hunter's door before entering." Mr. Lars De Luca is here to see you, Mr. Hunter."

Hunter thought for a moment about his last meeting with De Luca. "Give me five minutes, and then send him in."

The detective was, at first, cautiously optimistic at the possibility that De Luca stopped in with information about Abrielle. In retrospect, he had a hunch De Luca didn't make his way into his office with good intentions. After seeing her photo, De Luca made a positive ID of Abrielle, but was he there to tell what he knew about her?

Ingrid returned to her desk and noticed De Luca was seated but anxiously bouncing his leg and biting his nails. Then he made involuntary jerking movements with his arms. He began staring directly at her, so in an attempt to relax him, Ingrid started to ask if she could get him coffee or water, but he spoke over her by asking when he could see

De Luca, in his derangement, was destined to lead the order as its new messiah with the queen at his side. He would eliminate anyone who would prevent him from rebuilding the order's empire. He studied Hunter's business card one more time. *This must be the central operation of the order's persecutors. If I destroy the heart, I destroy the body, and a new era will begin!* De Luca conspired as his mind was raced.

When detective Hunter stepped into the waiting room, he wasn't surprised at De Luca's erratic behavior, considering their last meeting. "Mr. De Luca? I wasn't expecting you. Step into my office so we can talk."

Both men entered the office, and Hunter closed the door. When he turned around, De Luca had pulled out a concealed kitchen knife and darted toward the detective. He quickly grabbed De Luca's arm and disarmed him. Hunter, who had a fifth-degree black belt, then pinned Lars down. Hearing the commotion, Ingrid rushed into the room. She turned back to call the police, but Hunter ordered her to wait.

"But he attacked you!" Ingrid cried out.

"Wait twenty minutes and then call the police," Hunter instructed. He grilled De Luca until the police arrived; he revealed nothing viable about Abrielle or her possible whereabouts.

De Luca was jailed at the local precinct but eventually transferred to a padded cell. He laughed hysterically at the temporary setback, then screeched in anger, for his confinement wasted valuable time. He reasoned that such an inconvenience would delay his rise to prominence. His queen would soon find where he was held, and she was not to be reckoned with. She would command he be freed and force the persecutors to suffer the ultimate price. De Luca remained in the mental facility and was never released.

CHAPTER NINETEEN

Kady spent the night at a rescue mission and was awakened at 5:00 am. She checked in the day before, which included filling out forms about who she was and where she was headed. Before she could get a bed, she was required to attend a religious service that she felt was demeaning, for the pastors were often from a different religion than her own. She had been homeless for the past year, and she often went two to three days without food. She was thankful for a serving of eggs and bacon that was provided.

She usually dreaded leaving the mission, especially when inclement weather, but this particular morning was different. The previous day, a man, who she first thought was a cop, had given her a fifty-dollar bill after she had given him some information. He said he wasn't a cop, showed her some ID, and introduced himself as a private investigator.

"Do you recognize the woman in this picture?" Hunter asked as he showed Katy the cash but kept it firmly in his grip. It was a high school senior photo. It was Abrielle's last one before she disappeared.

Kady eyed the money and then looked closely at the photo. In the picture, a teenage girl's eyes radiated in a way as if you could see in her soul that revealed that she would never allow life to break her. The image looked hauntingly similar of a very sad and bitter woman she knew. She was shocked at the idea, for it was starkly different than how Abrielle appeared in real-time, who had the look of a woman shattered by life. "Yeah, I've seen her. She stayed at the mission from time to time. I saw her in the food lines at a church near the corner of Martin Luther King intersection."

This was the first real lead that Hunter had in many months. "When was the last time you saw her?"

"It was over a month ago. That's all I know, mister."

"Where do you think she could be?"

"I didn't know her. I would just see her around, as I said." Kady knew Abrielle more than she revealed since the two had snorted and smoked meth on several occasions. She focused on the money that Hunter held in his hand as he stood silently waiting for her to say more. She feared he wouldn't pay her unless she gave more information. "Who knows where she went? She might be staying with family, or she may have left the city and gone south. Some do when it turns cold. You said you would pay me!"

After talking to Hunter, Kady was making her usual rounds of panhandling on the avenue where she saw Abrielle. They both surmised that Hunter was not a private investigator, as he claimed, but a cop. Abrielle became paranoid that she could still be arrested over the Xander debacle that seemed like a lifetime ago. Could the authorities be looking for her after all these years? How many had it been? She thought about these questions and feared it was just a matter of time before they would catch up with her. She had to plan to leave the area and go as far away as possible.

CHAPTER TWENTY

She stepped inside the store to get out of the heat. Then, Abrielle looked out the window facing the city street and noticed a man with a striking resemblance to someone from the distant past. She thought her mind must be playing tricks on her as it sometimes did. Years had passed since Max had kidnapped her, but she still imagined she saw him from time to time, but this time it was someone else. She watched the man as he walked farther away. He was wearing an expensive suit and was carrying a briefcase. She continued to observe until he entered the Penobscot Building. She hurried out of the store to follow, went inside the same building, and looked around until she found the building's directory on the wall. Abrielle searched through the list until she saw the name, *Sabastian Cassworth*.

Sabastian was on the top of his game. After many years of hard work and determination, he finally had the career and lifestyle he dreamed of. His career allowed him ample vacation time to travel first class to exotic lands worldwide He owned a large home in Rosedale Park, one of the most expensive neighborhoods in the greater metropolitan area of Detroit. Most of all, he loved his work and couldn't wait to arrive at his office each morning.

He walked to his office at the Penobscot building, avoiding the varied derelicts like every morning. From a distance, Sabastian noticed a new one, which prompted him to do a double-take. She seemed to be staring directly at him but turned away. He only had a partial view of her, but she looked hauntingly familiar. He persistently thought about her throughout the day, and he couldn't erase her from his mind. He felt they had met before but couldn't place her. His mind was fixed on her as he lay in bed that evening. He drifted off to sleep, but errant dreams of her image caused him to have hypnic jerks that awakened him repeatedly.

When Abrielle could, she would stay at a safe distance from Sabastian to observe him exiting the parking garage as he usually always did. He would then walk to the building where she assumed he worked. He was always sharply dressed in the latest style of suits and ties. He also wore no wedding ring, and she hoped that he would be her ticket to finally escape her situation, but she needed a plan. She had never loved or even cared about him. He was just a stepping stone to better things in bygone days. However, she remembered he truly loved her once, and true love never dies. She mischievously smiled how she had manipulated him and how he was under her control. She was confident she could do it again. She saved what cash she could that wasn't spent on her drug habit, earned from selling beverage containers she picked up from the streets and odd jobs. She would need to get some cosmetics samples from the department stores and pick the most sexy clothes she could find from a second-hand shop.

Victoria, a caseworker who took pity on Abrielle, tried to style her hair that was balding due to malnutrition. Abrielle was very guarded about her past but had confided with Victoria, a psychologist. She was fascinated with Abrielle's stories of grandeur from her past. She claimed she was once the queen of what she described as a "society of many thousands." If all goes well, she planned to reunite with a wealthy and successful boyfriend from her youth. Victoria thought she was a textbook example of megalomania.

Abrielle stared at herself in the mirror before applying her makeup. Looking back at her were her deep creases and wrinkles. She considered how many women embraced their wrinkles as a life well-lived. It had been so long since she had lived the life of pleasure. She had lost count of the years, and she was still existing between shelters and the streets. She was beginning to give up on herself and life. She became less motivated to maintain personal care, and her teeth were rotting due to poor oral hygiene.

She thought about Claudia and how she must have been leading a full and rewarding life. Abrielle's mind was racing as she bitterly reflected on her existence. Nothing had turned out the way she intended. She still felt resentment toward her parents for bringing her sister into the world. She pondered how her life would have turned out if Claudia had never been born. It had been a dominant force her entire life. She must shrug off these thoughts that still haunt her and switch her mind to Sabastian. He was her best hope to escape her current situation but was that true? Was he really her *best* hope? The word *best* wasn't in the equation. In reality, he was her only hope, for she had dropped to the bottom. He was her single solution to escape homelessness and return to a life of splendor. She knew he was her only chance, and it was a slim one.

* * * * * * * * * * * *

It was finally Monday morning, and Sabastian was out of bed before the alarm sounded as usual. He was excited about returning to his office after two days off. He raced down the basement, where he had an impressive gym for a quick workout. After a shower, he put on a new suit and admired himself as he practiced, out loud his presentation one more time. *Today, I'll close the Wesson account,* he confidently thought to himself. Sabastian felt a twinge of doubt as he stepped out of his car when he arrived at work. He took a deep breath before he began to make his way to his building. *I'll be fine*, he murmured.

He exited the parking garage and was on the sidewalk. He saw the same woman he noticed weeks before, which he couldn't get out of his head. Previously, she looked away when he saw her but this time, she held her gaze. She stood directly in his path as he got closer. His heart began to race, and he was breathing heavily. He thought about the bizarre dreams the night after seeing her last. There was something about her, but he couldn't wrap his head around why she made him react this way. Somehow, he knew her but from where?

"Hello Sabastian," Abrielle said softly when he was just mere steps away.

Her voice was unmistakable. Distant memories of a tormented love came roaring back, but he thought that surely that couldn't be. Abrielle had disappeared long ago. It had been over thirty years, but there she was. It was her voice. She was older, but there was something else, and it was very wrong. The Abrielle that he'd known so long ago toyed with his emotions, ruined his life, and then vanished. It took years of therapy to get over her.

"A-A-Abrielle?" Sabastian stuttered.

"Yes, Sabastian! You remembered. It's me, and I can't believe it's you!" She extended her arms out to hug him. "It's amazing seeing you after all this time. You look so nice!" Abrielle tried to act naturally. "We have much catching up to do."

For years, during and after his emotional breakdown, Sabastian prayed to see her again. He expected her to come back to him during each day, week, and month after her abrupt departure. She had returned, and he realized, at that instant, she was that homeless woman, or did he just think she was homeless? It didn't matter at that moment. When they hugged, his knees buckled and became suddenly blind to the decline in her physical appearance beyond her years. It was not just natural changes of getting older but a worn look. The woman that stood before him looked like a gross caricature of the girl he was in love with. To everyone else, she appeared to be a grotesque version of the stunningly beautiful creature who once drove him insane with sexual desire. However, as if he was under a spell, he saw the same beauty he had known during their youth. He felt God had answered his prayers. It just took him a while. God did it in his own time and in his infinite way. The infatuation he had for Abrielle, over three decades before, returned. It was as if she never left and who was he to question it?

CHAPTER TWENTY-ONE

Jonah, Sabastian's best friend and colleague, had always admired his friend's lifestyle. He was a natural at attracting the most beautiful women in the city. It was a gift that Sabastian was blessed with and what Jonah wanted. He anticipated meeting with Sabastian after his telephone call the night before. Sabastian had reunited with an old flame, and he claimed she was the love of his life. She was the one that got away but had come back. Jonah thought she must be extraordinarily hot. Up until then, Sabastian seemed to have a new girlfriend every few weeks and would never be tied down with just one.

Jonah was bewildered at the sight of Sabastian and Abrielle, who were sitting across the table, kissing and cuddling like adolescents. Such behavior seemed out of character for Sabastian, who had a square-toed type personality. He had explained that he had known Abrielle from his teenage years. To Jonah, the couple seems like a mismatch from hell. He knew Sabastian to be a true professional in his field and was meticulous in his appearance and with the women he was seen with. He thought the woman Sabastian was with, dressed, and smelled like a street person. Jonah's date, Stella, who accompanied him, felt the scene was hilarious.

Giddy with excitement, Sabastian shared how he and Abrielle reunited after thirty years apart. His story was a repeat of a rambling telephone discussion with Jonah the evening before.

Is this a joke? Jonah wondered this since Sabastian had been known to pull some creative but harmless pranks at the office. He would occasionally place a penny under one's coffee mug and then later under the same coworker's mouse, just for fun. Why would he go to such extremes as to pick a homeless person off the street for a put-on? What could he possibly expect to get out of it? He studied Sabastian to detect any pretense. Jonah seized on the opportunity to ask him when Abrielle excused herself to visit the restroom. Stella got up to follow and find out more about her. She was an attorney by profession and could get the truth from people. However, she was amazed at Abrielle's story, which seemed very convincing about her relationship with Sabastian.

"Bravo! You've pulled some good ones in the past, but this time, you've outdone yourself, but I don't get it," Jonah suggested to Sabastian. "What's up?"

"What's up? What on earth are you talking about, Jonah?"

Jonah looked back in astonishment. "That woman. That's what I'm talking about—that bag lady you brought in here. I appreciate a good gag as much as anyone, but this is a stretch, don't you think? What's going on?"

Sabastian was, at first, dumbfounded and then became angry. "Listen, Jonah. I've known you for a long time. Well enough to realize you're jealous of me, but you don't have to get cute. You're being very disrespectful to Abrielle. I thought better of you. What the hell are you doing?" He shouted. The other diners were looking over their way.

"You can stop the performance. You've gone too far. You're making a scene, and you're out of line, my friend."

At that moment, the women were walking back to their table. Sabastian stood, took Abrielle by the arm, and left the restaurant.

"What was that all about, and why are we leaving? I'm hungry!" Abrielle asked confusingly. She had already ordered the largest cut of filet mignon, and now they were leaving.

"Jonah and I got into a disagreement about a work project but don't worry, darling. We'll go to another and even better restaurant. I'll fix things with Jonah tomorrow." Sabastian didn't want her to know the truth about Jonah's remarks.

Abrielle was surprised that Sabastian was not only interested in her after many years; he seemed to be head-over-heels in love. Her plan had worked beyond her wildest dreams. It had been three days, and he naturally asked questions about her livelihood and where she lived. She was not ready to reveal she hadn't worked in years and was homeless, so she told him that her company had recently downsized. She left her position as a designer to search for another in the city, when they met. Sabastian had not changed in some ways, for he swallowed every lie she shoveled out, just like he did in the old days. Although she had declined to the lowest depths in life and he had reached great heights, Abrielle still felt nothing intimately for Sabastian. She only needed a way out of her current situation, and she had been trying to break away from the cocaine before it was too late.

Sabastian was outraged, but he was earnestly confused at Jonah's remarks about Abrielle. To tease playfully when someone falls in love is sometimes expected among friends. They knew one another's habits and strengths, and each could often enjoy laughs at the expense of the other. Jonah's behavior was over-the-top and made no sense. Nicholas stewed in silence while waiting for a parking valet at *Bernie's,* an upscale restaurant at Grand River Avenue. He hoped it would appease Abrielle after their abrupt departure from the other restaurant. He knew how excited she was about dining out and enjoying a night on the town. He couldn't resist showing her off, so he invited Jonah and Stella to meet them at the restaurant. Surely, it was just Jealousy for Jonah's awkward behavior. *Poor Jonah never had much luck with women*, Sabastian mused.

CHAPTER TWENTY-TWO

Abrielle was fully rested for the first time in a long stretch after sleeping under silk sheets on Sabastian's king-size bed. She was used to lying on sidewalks and park benches but sometimes was fortunate enough to enjoy the luxury of resting on a shelter bed. Sleeping on a real mattress was like heaven. Before leaving for work, Sabastian lay a stash of bills on the nightstand for Abrielle to spend as she chose. He also left her a car to drive and asked that she come to his office later. He was anxious to introduce her to his colleagues and show her off. She stared at the cash and tried to resist her urge to use it to buy drugs. Sabastian's help was her ticket to escape her lonely existence. She grabbed the money, got ready, and headed out the door.

* * * * * * * * * * *

For Sabastian, it was like walking back in time to his youth. Abrielle not only returned to him, but she was also living in his home just like old times. He excitedly anticipated her visit to his office. He was jubilant about reuniting with Abrielle and sharing his new life with everyone on his team. He was usually guarded with his personal life up until then. He continued to gloat the morning away to everyone but Jonah, whom he spurned disdainfully. Jonah sat silently at his desk but still at a loss over the woman that Sabastian had brought to the restaurant. Jonah could hear almost everything that Sabastian was uttering through the walls of the cubicles. *Did Sabastian say that the bag lady was coming to the office? This is going to be interesting,* thought Jonah.

Stepping out of Sabastian's car, Abrielle had the shakes and was desperate to score a hit. Her addiction made her paranoid, and she couldn't stop thinking about the cop, who Kady warned her about. To make it worse, Sabastian was driving her bananas. She was glad that he still cared for her and allowed her to stay with him. He treated her like royalty, but his constant fixation with her was intolerable. Nonetheless, she had to please him for a while, and that meant going to his workplace, as he had been pestering her to do. First, she needed a fix to get through it, which meant going to the inner city where she feared the cop would be lurking around.

* * * * * * * * * * * *

Blair loved being a receptionist. After graduating from high school, some of her classmates took summer jobs at auto plants or steel mills. However, Blair felt lucky to land a comfortable temporary position working inside the Penobscot building before starting college. Best of all, she had a crush on Sabastian, an executive in her office. The way he greeted Blair each morning made her melt. She knew her chances of dating him were impossible, for it violated the rules of conduct that she swore to uphold during her orientation. It was rumored that Sabastian was compared to Casanova because it seemed like he had a new girlfriend every week. His current one, who he referred to as *Abrielle,* must have been special for he was telling all the staff about her. His private life was a subject he had never discussed before. He informed Blair that she would be stopping by for a visit, and she was anxious to meet her, the girl who finally stole Sabastian's heart.

Blair was sheltered by her parents while growing up in Grosse Point, one of the wealthiest suburbs in the Detroit area. So, she was shocked at the vagrants who roamed the streets outside her workplace, and they made her nervous while walking from the parking garage. She would pass by at least one beggar almost every morning going to the Penobscot building or leaving every evening. When a woman she recognized as one of the frequent street dwellers walked into the receptionist room, Blair was prepared to call security because she thought the woman must be there to panhandle. The woman reeked of alcohol, and she wasn't sure how to handle the situation.

"You shouldn't be in here!" Blair admonished.

"But Sabastian, who works here, asked me to come," replied Abrielle.

"Sabastian? You mean you're Abrielle?"

"Yeah, I'm her." Abrielle almost wished the girl behind the small desk would refuse to allow her to enter, but she felt committed to doing as Sabastian asked. She had his car for the day, and he gave her a thousand dollars to buy clothes or anything that pleased her. She wanted to stay in his good graces, but she considered running off and leaving him after counting the money. If she stayed around a little longer, she could get her hands on more of Sabastian's money. The last place she wanted to be was at his work and meeting his coworkers. She had contemplated coping a hit of meth to help her get geared up but held back, for she was determined to quit for good. Instead, she bought a bottle of bourbon, and she sat in the parking lot, intending to take only a couple of sips to build up her courage before going in. One sip led to another, and she drank most of the bottle.

In utter bafflement, Blair was at a loss what to do next. She was new and only received a minimal amount of training. As the receptionist, part of her responsibility was to be the gatekeeper. She was instructed to deter all who didn't have an appointment. She was told that usually, the only visitors who requested to see any staff without an appointment were salesmen. She wasn't sure if the woman was who she said. After all, she was one of the beggars she had seen on the avenue and was obviously drunk. Blair didn't want to make the wrong decision, but Sabastian had said earlier that his newest girlfriend was the love of his life and he had always regretted losing her long ago but magically was in his life, again.

"Why don't you have a seat, Abrielle, and I'll call Sabastian to tell him you're here."

Seconds after Blare called Sabastian; he swiftly made his way to the reception room. "You're just in time, my darling," Sabastian said to Abrielle as he caressed her. "It's almost lunchtime. I hope you're hungry. I'll take you to a little restaurant that's the best in the city for lunch. First, I want you to meet the gang. I see you've met Blair."

"We've met," Blair replied, nonplussed.

"Hey there," Abrielle slurred the words as she placed her hand on Blair's desk for balance.

Sabastian led her to the partitioned office area, and they stopped at each cubicle for introductions. Humphrey had a reputation for spreading malicious gossip about his coworkers and flattering his superiors. He was known as the office brown nose, lackey, bootlicker, and more formally, sycophant. He peeked over the wall of his cubicle to observe Sabastian stopping by each unit with an odd-looking woman. Her appearance and behavior aroused his curiosity enough to ease out of his office domain to get closer so he could listen to what was going on. He was still bitter over the time Sabastian had received a lucrative account that was rightfully his. Humphrey first thought that Sabastian was escorting her around to collect donations to help her with some financial aid. He smiled cynically when he discovered the real reason for her visit. Several others popped their heads up over their cubicle walls to get a look as the whispers became louder. Waiting no longer, Humphrey walked over to introduce himself.

"Looks like you got yourself quite a catch, Sabastian!" Humphrey mockingly praised as he extended his hand to meet Abrielle. The stench of a musky second-hand store reached his nostrils. He took her hand that felt rough, and the skin was dry and cracked. Her face was weathered, and one of her eye teeth was missing.

"I'm a lucky man, for sure," boasted Sabastian.

Others gathered around as Sabastian, jovially explained, in detail, how they met. Their fixed eyes on her made Abrielle feel uncomfortable, and she became dizzy from the unwanted attention mixed with the alcohol she earlier consumed.

"What's wrong, darling? Are you feeling sick?" Sabastian asked worriedly.

"I'll be fine. I need to go now." She turned to walk out with Sabastian trailing while the others stared in stunned silence. Abrielle had reached her breaking point. She couldn't tolerate being around him much longer regardless of the security he could offer her. She remembered how pathetic he was when they were young, but the years apart did nothing to improve his demeanor. Surviving on the street was better than trying to tolerate his obsession over her.

When Sabastian returned home that evening, Abrielle was gone, and she didn't come in until midnight. Agitated and twitching from the meth she had consumed all evening caused her to be in no mood to deal with Sabastian over her whereabouts.

The following day Abrielle was apologetic for the previous evening but offered no explanation. Terrified that he was losing her, Sabastian told her he had decided to add her name to his savings account in desperation to conciliate.

The following morning, he received a text message from Sidney, the department manager. Sid instructed Sabastian to report to him upon his arrival at the office.

* * * * * * * * * * * *

"What in hell is going on, Sabastian?" Sidney asked angrily.

"I don't know what you mean. Everything is fine."

"Who was that woman you paraded around yesterday?"

"That was Abrielle. She's my girl. Why?" As his captivation for Abrielle deepened, he could no longer grasp basic job-related principles.

"Your girl? Do you want to try again?"

"No, I do not." Sabastian remained adamant.

Sidney looked at him doubtfully. "Regardless of who she is, you know the rules. It's a violation of the company's code of conduct to have anyone not affiliated with the company in the workplace!"

"Under normal circumstances, I agree with the rule."

"Under no circumstances! I don't want to hear any more complaints about you bringing your *girl* in here, again. I don't have time for this. Now, get out of here."

The others tried to act natural when Sabastian walked out of Sidney's office. Humphrey peeked over his cubicle with a self-serving smirk.

After leaving work, Sabastian was unperturbed by his confrontation with Sidney. He stopped at a jewelry store to pick up an engagement ring he had ordered and at a florist for a dozen red roses. It was the night he would propose to Abrielle, and he wanted everything to be perfect before uttering those four critical words. He didn't want to just blurt out the words. He wanted to tell her what marriage meant to him and why she was the one for him. He had been going over it in his mind the whole day.

He was so excited when he got home that he did a little happy dance before walking through the door as he held the roses. He called her name, but she didn't answer. He checked every room and the pool area. He tried calling her cell he'd given to her and then a text but no response. Not knowing what to do next, he sat on the sofa as he clutched his cell and waited. An hour had passed, then two. He tried to call and texted her several times. He remembered there were some photo prints inside the end table drawer. He took them out and looked at each one. Almost all were shots of him and Abrielle on their recent excursions. He opened his laptop and downloaded her images. He searched until he found one of his favorites and expanded it until it was lifelike. He was amazed at how stunning she still looked, and he thought how little her appearance had changed throughout the years. He grimaced at all that wasted time they could have been together. He was so engrossed with the pictures that the sound of the ringtone, indicating a text message on his cell, startled him. It was a notification from his bank. He opened the website that revealed a large withdrawal from earlier that day. He thought it must have been a glitch in the computer system, so he called the bank's automated system that confirmed the notification. After the initial shock, he realized that Abrielle had taken all the money from the account. He thought she must have had a plausible reason. He was confident she would come home, explain what happened, and everything would be ok, so he waited.

The sunlight peeking through the open blind awakened Sabastian. He called out for Abrielle, hoping she would come home during the night. He checked his cell for messages. He tried not to jump to conclusions as he sat on the sofa to think. He rationalized why she was still gone and what possessed her to clean out the account. It wasn't all his money but just a smaller account for her personal use. Perhaps she was kidnapped, and her assailant forced her to withdraw the cash. The kidnappers would call and demand more money. He considered calling the police to report her missing but thought how foolish he would feel if she returned safely on her own. He fought his emotions at the thought she may have left intentionally and made off with the money he had entrusted with her. The photos he was looking at during the night were scattered on the lampstand, and some had fallen to the floor. He picked one up and noticed an image of someone who should have been Abrielle but wasn't. He picked up more photos with the image of the same woman, who was Abrielle but drastically different. The person seemed to have some vague physical similarities but a haggard appearance. In disbelief, he realized his mind had played tricks on him all along. His first sight of her and how she had changed was too much for him to accept. His subconscious took over, and within his mind, he saw Abrielle the way she was long ago. He realized then that she was gone. His heartbreak would be never-ending, nor would he ever love again.

CHAPTER TWENTY-THREE

He could have given her security and a comfortable life. These things had been hopelessly out of Abrielle's reach, but she couldn't tolerate Sabastian's smothering any longer. In any case, with the money that she took from his bank account, she could have the life she desired without him. Even better, she could have the life she once had before, when many idolized her. *Idolized?* Was that really true, and how long had it been since anyone actually admired her but Sabastian? She concluded that such thoughts were gibberish, and she began having misgivings about leaving him so hastily. He only had a few thousand dollars in the account. Realistically, not enough to provide for herself very long, especially considering her drug addiction.

Regardless, she couldn't go back. It's too late for that. She had spoiled the possibility of returning to him when she took the money. She wisely left Sabastian's car and cell phone that he provided her in his garage. Both could be traced, and she didn't want to be found. She called a taxi from Sabastian's home, but when the dispatcher asked for her destination, she was momentarily stumped. She couldn't go back to the inner city of Detroit, for that's where the police, or she thought, was looking for her.

"I need a ride to the bus depot," Abrielle replied to the dispatcher.

She considered writing a *Dear John Letter,* for she felt she owed Sabastian that much, at least. However, the taxi had already arrived and was waiting. A letter to reveal the bad news of ending their relationship didn't apply to Abrielle. For her, it wasn't that type of connection, for she was only using him. When she got inside the taxi, she looked back one last time. Doubt was gnawing away at her decision.

* * * * * * * * * * *

"Why do I need a picture ID? I just need to get to Chicago." Abrielle pleaded with the bus terminal attendant.

"It's US Department rules, ma'am. The attendant replied that all passengers must submit a photo ID before getting on our buses," the attendant replied.

"I lost all my identification and I have to get on that bus. Can't you make an exception?"

"Sorry, but no picture ID, no bus ticket. It's still early, so why don't you go to the *Secretary of State* and get another. Have a seat while I take care of the rest of the passengers, and then I'll get you the address. Our bus schedules to Chicago run every three hours, day and night. You can catch one this evening, but you must have an ID."

Applying for valid identification through Michigan's Secretary of State or any agency was impossible, for she still feared arrest. A thudding that she recognized as her heartbeat echoed in her ears at the thought of Kady telling her about the detective, who was snooping around and asking questions about her. So, Abrielle decided she must stay in hiding.

The taxi driver sat at the cab stand adjacent to the bus station. Derelicts didn't often ask for his service, but when they did, they would offer a barter such as cheap costume jewelry or other trinkets in exchange. He was reluctant to yield Abrielle a ride until she presented him with cash for fare to prove she could pay. With nowhere else to go, she had the driver take her to the inner city. It was only there that she had connections with people she knew who could provide her with drugs for her substance use. She had been determined to quit, but the addiction was too powerful. For each dose, she vowed to stop for good, but the withdrawals would begin tormenting her just hours afterward and would last for days. A crash marked the onslaught of the withdrawals. Whenever she wasn't feeling the effects of the high that she received on cocaine, she would return to thoughts of Claudia, and her feeling of worthlessness would follow.

Gaining access to the internet while staying with Sabastian, Abrielle could click on any search engine to pull up a wealth of information about her sister. In her search, she discovered how Claudia was enjoying immense success as a nationally known attorney. She had the kind of life of what dreams were made of. Her husband, Brent, was CEO of a prosperous industrial enterprise. They had a son and daughter who were students in an ivy league college. Abrielle would seethe with envy that would plunge her into depression, and her only escape was when she was high. Cocaine would give her a feeling of power, confidence, and energy.

* * * * * * * * * * *

"I've reviewed your sister's entire case, and it's the most mysterious one in our file," expressed Detective Sylvester Hunter to Claudia. Sylvester had taken over his father's agency when he retired. "As you know, we have been on the trail of a woman who could or not be Abrielle. There is evidence of both."

"How likely could it be that she's my sister?" Claudia asked as she grabbed Brent's hand to brace herself for the detective's answer. Her husband had remained supportive throughout the years, but he inwardly had extreme doubts that Abrielle would ever be found and the enormous expense involved. After the death of their parents, Claudia leaned heavily on Brent for support. As Bethany lay on the hospital bed, stricken with cancer, she made Claudia promise never to give up looking for Abrielle. After losing her father to a fatal heart attack, the year before, it was just too soon for Claudia to lose her mother too.

"We won't know until I find this person, and it has momentarily gone cold." He was astounded that the family still wanted to continue the search after thirty-five years. The investigator was drawn to the case after researching the events that led his father on an incredible journey. As elusive as the case had become, it was as if the hard-to-find Abrielle was an actual phantom. He had considered advising the family to stop the search, for it was becoming more apparent that the subject didn't want to be found. He also considered the possibility that she was dead, but who was the woman that his father had been following if that was true? Sylvester had to know, somehow or other, for he was so intrigued that he would continue the search for as long as the family desired.

* * * * * * * * * * *

With all of the money gone that Abrielle took from Sabastian's account, she was desperate for more coke. Suffering from tremors, shakiness, and chills, she found herself several City blocks from the nearest shelter. Overwhelmed by her depressive circumstances and loneliness, she walked aimlessly. She fell on the sidewalk and almost lost consciousness. She realized she was only a few yards from a church. She looked around and was thankful no police cars were approaching. She picked herself up and made her way to the church steps to sit and rest. She heard singing coming from inside, and she remembered hearing the song when she attended church as a young girl. The name of it was *It is Well with My Soul*. Memories of her youth came flooding back, and she wept. She missed her family, but they were a foregone conclusion, for she had not seen them in decades.

She shrugged off thoughts of the past to focus on her immediate survival plan. She had to get back to her familiar domain, where she could find shelter for the night. It was almost dark, and she didn't have enough money for bus fare. She saw a well-dressed couple who had walked past her. They were holding hands, and they seemed very happy. They kept walking and turned to climb the steps leading to the church entrance. This was Abrielle's chance to ask the couple for the bus fare. *They're church people,* she reasoned. *Surely, they will help.* The city bus passed by every thirty minutes, and she couldn't lose her chance.

"Sir?" Abrielle spoke out to the well-dressed man. "Can you spare me enough change for bus fare, please?"

The couple turned to look back at Abrielle. She was in utter disbelief when she saw the stylishly dressed woman face to face and turned to run away when she realized it was her sister. Likewise, Claudia recognized Abrielle and shouted out to her.

"Abrielle! Please…is it you?" She stopped but kept her head turned away in shame. "Oh, Abrielle, I can't believe it's you! Where have you been all this time?"

Overwhelmed with humiliation, all she could say was that she was sorry, as she kept her head down and tried to hide her face.

Brent spoke up as it began to rain. "Let's all go inside the church to get out of this weather."

He and Claudia were on each side of Abrielle and guided her by her arms. Once inside, the two women embraced. They looked at one another in stunned surprise. It was Wednesday night prayer service, and fewer members than usual were present. They entered the auditorium and sat on the back pew as the parishioners continued singing. The pastor stood to take prayer requests as Abrielle and Claudia quietly talked. Toward the end of the service, the pastor commenced with an altar call for anyone to come before the congregation who wished to show their commitment. The sisters stood and held hands as they made their way to the altar.

www.ingramcontent.com/pod-product-compliance
Lightning Source LLC
LaVergne TN
LVHW041850070526
838199LV00045BB/1527